Alice tr
but he was too strong . . .

The killer had Alice's right arm in a grip so tight each finger was outlined in white. It looked grotesque, since his hand was sheathed in a thin rubber glove. His face was twisted into a snarl of triumph and something else. She struggled, but he only clenched more tightly. Then she saw what was in his other hand—a tire iron.

She cried out as his fingers bit deeper into her arm. The tire iron came up, and Alice closed her eyes. It was inches from crushing her skull.

Read these terrifying thrillers
from HarperPaperbacks!

Sweet Dreams
Sweetheart
Teen Idol
Running Scared
by Kate Daniel

And don't miss M. C. Sumner's
horrifying new trilogy

The Principal
The Substitute *
The Coach *

* coming soon

Baby-sitter's Nightmare

Kate Daniel

HarperPaperbacks
A Division of HarperCollins*Publishers*

HarperPaperbacks *A Division of* HarperCollins*Publishers*
10 East 53rd Street, New York, N.Y. 10022

Copyright © 1992 by Kate Daniel
and Daniel Weiss Associates, Inc.
Cover art copyright © 1992 by Daniel Weiss
Associates, Inc.

Produced by Daniel Weiss Associates, Inc.
33 West 17th Street, New York, New York 10011.

First printing: April 1992

Printed in the United States of America

HarperPaperbacks and colophon are trademarks of
HarperCollins*Publishers*

10 9 8 7 6 5

For Susan Shwartz,
who started it all.

"Everybody blame Susan!"

ONE

Alice Fleming leaned back against the door, inhaling deeply to keep from letting out a yell of triumph. Classes wouldn't let out for another ten minutes, and she really shouldn't disturb them. But it was hard to keep quiet when she wanted to shout the good news at the top of her voice. She'd done it! She was going to get the Community Aid Scholarship.

Alice straightened up and started walking slowly toward her locker. She didn't want to go back to class; it would be impossible to concentrate on American history right now. Mrs. Komax, the school counselor, had given her a hallpass and suggested she get ready to leave. Alice was grinning to herself as she walked down the corridor. Mrs. Komax had been almost as delighted as Alice herself. She knew how long and how hard Alice had worked toward her dream of going to a good university.

Alice had always known it would be up to her; the Flemings didn't have the money to pay for a top college. Even though her grades were among the highest in the senior class, she'd never really expected to win the Community Aid Scholarship. It was special—only one was awarded each year. Like most scholarships, it was based in part on need and in part on grades. But it also recognized determination and potential worth and service. The Community Aid Scholarship said that Anslow, Colorado, thought that Alice was a credit to the community. The honor was worth as much as the scholarship itself.

Almost. Alice grinned again, thinking about the college catalogs cluttering her room at home. Her dream school was now within reach. Of course, Mrs. Komax had explained there were still some formalities to go through. Alice was an item on the agenda of the next meeting of the Anslow City Council. Once they voted to name her the recipient, the state committee would send her the certificate.

Alice balanced her stack of text books in one hand and pulled open her locker with the other.

Only a couple assignments for this evening, she decided, shoving most of the books onto the top shelf of the locker. As she slammed the metal door shut, the final bell rang. The instant noise signaling the end of the school day gave her the excuse she needed. She let out a yell of pure triumph.

A moment later, it was answered by a male voice.

"Hey, babe." Ryan Derosa moved up behind her and put an arm around her shoulder. "You look happy. What did Komax have for you, something good?"

"The best. Ryan, I'm getting the Community Service!" Alice bubbled over.

"Hey, that's great!" Ryan smiled down at her, his eyes dancing mischievously. "Proves how smart *I* am, too. Takes a smart guy to grab the smartest girl in school. And the prettiest." He slid his hands down to her waist and started to pick her up, but they were both nearly knocked off their feet as the boy at the next locker slammed into them. "No Athletic Club tonight," Ryan said. "You ready to go?"

They started out toward the parking lot, arms around each other's waists. "Want to go into Pueblo tonight for dinner, celebrate a little? We can try that fancy place Rita was telling me about."

Alice shook her head, letting her long blond hair swing forward. "I can't. It's Tuesday; I have to sit for the Munsons."

"C'mon, missing one time won't kill them. Besides, the scholarship takes care of the money worries, doesn't it? So live a little." They reached his convertible and dumped their books in the back. "Look, we can drop by your place, you phone her, and get ready. Simple."

Alice got in, while Ryan went around to the driver's side. As usual he didn't bother opening the door; he just dropped his six-foot frame over the side. Instead of starting the car he slid an arm around her shoulders and pulled her over against him.

"You'd love it. Rita said it was the best food she's had since last summer in San Francisco. What the heck, we could go someplace afterward, make it a real party. Skip school tomorrow if we get home too late. Your grades won't be hurt by missing a day, and mine are beyond help anyway." He smiled at his final half-truth and finished very softly: "Want to?"

It was so hard saying no to him. "Ryan, I want to, but I can't tonight. The Munsons have been out of town, and I can't leave them without a sitter on their first night back."

"You can't disappoint the Munsons, but you can disappoint me?" Ryan put a finger under the tip of her chin and raised her head so she had to look him in the eyes. As she started to protest, he leaned forward and gave her a quick kiss. "Relax. I understand. We'll celebrate later in the week, okay? Unless you don't have any free nights."

"I'll have a free night. And I do want to celebrate. But I have to be at the Munsons an hour from now."

"Okay. Until then, we can go for a ride. I'll take you over there, but you owe me a night out. With no sitting."

He backed the car out of its slot, gravel spurting as he gunned the engine. He was handling the car with the automatic ease he showed at most things. As they headed out of the parking lot, Alice looked at him, wondering again how she'd ever lucked into a guy like Ryan. They'd been dating for a month now, the most exciting month of her life. His dark eyes and black hair were such a vivid contrast to her own pale blond hair and blue eyes. They made a striking couple, or so she'd been told. She didn't care about what they looked like, though.

She was just glad to be part of a couple with Ryan.

Almost too glad. Alice was a little afraid of the intensity of her feelings. It wasn't just that he was so good-looking. It was the way he always seemed so self-possessed and in control of any situation. Maybe it was easy to be in control when you never had to ask twice for anything. Ryan's family had money; they were among the wealthiest in town. It gave him a slight edge of sophistication and arrogance that Alice found fascinating. It wasn't easy to remember real life when you were dating Prince Charming.

Ryan didn't understand Alice's baby-sitting, though. Since he'd never had to work for anything, he couldn't understand how important college was to Alice. She'd been baby-sitting for years, saving every penny and knowing it still wasn't enough. Now she had the scholarship, but she couldn't slack off. The scholarship would cover tuition, but room, board, and books would still be expensive. Ryan didn't have to worry about stuff like that. His folks would pay for it, and it would come as easily as his car had. Alice hated to admit it, but Ryan was spoiled.

And no question, it was easy to get spoiled. Alice didn't want to go back to walking or riding her bike. It was so much nicer being chauffeured by Ryan in his screaming-yellow convertible. Even when his driving left her shaking.

"Ryan, could you slow down?" Alice didn't want to be late getting to the Munsons', and if Ryan was stopped again for speeding she would be. They were out of town now, and the wind from the lowered top was making her hair whip around like a flag. "You can't afford another ticket, anyway. What if you lost your license?"

He laughed, but slowed down anyway. "Never happen, babe. My dad had a little talk with the chief last time. They might pull me over, but I'd have to be really wasted or something before they'd give me a ticket."

"He bribed them?"

"Alice, this isn't Wonderland, remember?" He had picked up the Wonderland jokes her family had always shared, so appropriate with her looks and name. "That's how the world works, Alice. But no, I didn't mean Dad gave him a bribe. They just got the idea it would be a waste of time hassling me anymore; make 'em look bad. Tell you what, though; as a special treat, I'll drive real slow. That'll give us more time together anyway."

He suited his actions to his words, slowing almost to a crawl. "When will you get the official word on the scholarship? You said something about the city council needing to do something."

"Ms. Komax said they'll meet next week. But they wouldn't have scheduled it unless they'd made up their minds. You know I decided I was going to go to Colorado College back when I was in second grade? I don't think I'll really believe I'm there until after the first semester."

"If I know you, you'll be too busy baby-sitting to get money for graduate school to even notice college." That comment stung a bit, but there was some truth to it.

"I promise I won't ever be too busy baby-sitting to go out with you when we're at C.C. I just have to get there first."

"Alice, I may not be going to C.C. after all." Ryan was turning onto the lake road as he spoke and didn't see the stricken look on Alice's face. "They've been getting a little sticky about grade-point averages and all that garbage."

"But . . . I thought we'd both be at Colorado College." Alice tried to keep her voice light. She wasn't ready to give up Ryan. Suddenly the eight months left in the school year seemed too short. Abruptly, she changed the subject, not wanting to think about the future.

"When your dad was talking to the chief, did he say anything about the break-ins?"

"No, we've got a good enough alarm system; Dad doesn't worry about it. Besides, insurance would cover it if anything happened. I'll bet the chief thought Dad was going to blast him about it. When you have a lot of burglaries in a hicksville town like this, where the cops are too dumb to catch a cold, you figure the people with something to lose are going to squawk."

Ryan's family wasn't the only one with something to lose. The first few break-ins hadn't done much damage, and the thieves hadn't stolen much, but lately they'd been vandalizing as well as stealing anything light, portable, and salable. Not all of the households were well-to-do, either.

At first, there had been jokes about a crime wave in sleepy little Anslow. Then people had started to get mad. Now some people were calling it a Reign of Terror. That was an exaggeration, but fear was growing, along with the tension of waiting to see who would be hit next.

"Yesterday, the *Answer* said the police had a new lead," Alice said.

Ryan snorted. "The *Anslow Answer* never even knows the question and you know it, Alice. Saying they have a lead is automatic. The police would say that no matter what."

"I'm not so sure. Anyway, we'd better start back into town. It's almost time for me to be at the Munsons'."

"Don't see why they couldn't have stayed out of town another few days." He pulled off the road and turned the car around, then kissed her before starting back into town. "If they'd been considerate enough to stay gone, we could head for the city right now."

"We'll get to that restaurant soon. I like the places Rita finds. They're sure expensive, though."

He shrugged. "Doesn't matter. I just wanted more time with you. Between the books and the baby-sitting, I see less of you than any girl I've ever gone out with."

Ryan headed the car back into Anslow, and the talk shifted to other things.

Too quickly, they pulled up in front of the Munsons' house. Ryan reached behind them to retrieve her books from the back seat. As she got out, she heard a yell. Tyler Munson was running toward them across the lawn, his eyes opened wide.

"Alice! Hey Alice, betcha can't guess what happened to us!"

She smiled; Tyler was one of her favorites. "I don't know . . . you had a great trip and you've got something to show me? Right?"

Tyler shook his head. His eyes were still wide, and she suddenly realized he looked frightened.

"Somebody robbed us!"

TWO

Alice scrambled out of the car. She gave Tyler a quick hug, then got her books from Ryan. For the first time, she noticed the police cars, one in the driveway and a second across the street. Ryan gave her a fast hug, then drove off, gunning the engine a little as if in salute to the squad cars.

Alice followed Tyler toward the house. Incomprehensible static squawks were blasting from the police radio in the car. As they walked into the living room, Alice immediately had the unreal feeling of watching a TV program, as several police officers moved around, taking photographs, making notes, checking rooms. Mrs. Munson was sitting on the sofa, or what was left of it. Judging from the slashed fabric and gaping cuts, someone had ripped it up with a knife. Stuffing bulged from the ruptured pillows, and little wisps of it drifted around the room like dandelion fluff. Alice remembered how happy Mrs. Munson had been when she'd gotten the new furniture, six months before.

Tyler shrank back, pushing against Alice's leg. Normally, he was as allergic to "mushy stuff" as any healthy seven-year-old boy, but this wasn't a normal day. Alice slipped an arm around his shoulder and guided him toward the family room. With luck, it would be free of the confusion enveloping the rest of the house.

Luck, however, was something the Munsons were out of right now. Alice stopped on the threshold of the family room. Little ceramic statuettes—souvenirs of various state and national parks visited over many years of vacations—lay in shards on the floor. The knicknacks were valueless in terms of money, but Alice knew how much they meant to Mrs. Munson. There couldn't have been any real reason to destroy them. Just senseless cruelty by someone who thought it was fun to break things.

Alice's grip on Tyler's shoulders tightened slightly as she steered him back to the living room. They sat down in the window seat, where they'd be out of the way but able to see what was going on. Tyler looked half scared and half excited. Alice couldn't blame him. Burglaries looked exciting on TV. But in real life, they were pretty frightening.

"Where's your dad, Tyler?"

"He was supposed to stay away an extra day. Mom called him, and I could hear him yelling on the phone. He's coming home now. Mom had to call the cops and everything, and she said I shouldn't even go in my own room."

"Are you scared?" Alice kept her arm lightly around Tyler's shoulders while she tried to see what was happening in the confusion. Across the room Mrs. Munson had been joined on the couch by a man in a business suit.

"Who, me?" Tyler hesitated for a moment, then the fear won out over the little boy bravado. "A little, I guess. I'll be glad when Dad gets home. Mom cried when she saw her stuff all broken up in there. Why'd they do that, Alice?"

"I don't know, Tyler. I have no idea why someone would want to do this. Think maybe we could clean it up some?"

The man in the suit answered her. Alice had been speaking softly, but he seemed to notice everything. "Please don't touch anything, miss."

Despite the "please," it was clearly an order. "Mrs. Munson, is this young woman a relative?"

"No, she's our baby-sitter, Alice Fleming. Alice, this is Detective Higgins." It felt strange, being formally introduced in the middle of a crisis. "Oh, Alice, can you believe this?" She started to cry once more, and Tyler went over and hugged her.

"I'm so sorry, Mrs. Munson. Can I take Tyler on a walk, maybe? Fix him some supper?"

Again, the detective answered. "Please. I'd prefer it if you remained here in case we need to ask you any questions. From what Mrs. Munson said, I assume you work here frequently?"

"Every Tuesday for four hours, usually. Sometimes on other days as well."

Mrs. Munson added, "Alice has been our sitter for over two years. Tyler adores her." Tyler, predictably, objected loudly to this mush. They went back to the window seat while the questioning continued. She heard Higgins ask who had known they'd be out of town. Alice knew it hadn't been in the papers. Mrs. Munson had said many times gossip-page articles on vacations and trips were just an invitation to thieves. These thieves hadn't waited for the invitation.

A few minutes later a news truck for the local television station pulled up in front of the house. Alice lost track of Detective Higgins's questioning while she tried to keep Tyler under control. He wanted to go outside and be on television. Convincing him it would upset his mother took some time, but he finally gave up. Kneeling on the window seat, Tyler pressed his nose firmly against the glass and watched the mysterious doings of the TV truck. The police were no longer the most interesting thing in the universe.

Alice kept her eye on Tyler, but couldn't help overhearing the detective.

". . . when it happened. That's the pattern; there are only a couple of these jobs we can pin down to a narrow enough time span to make it worth checking alibis. Are you sure you can't think of anyone else who knew you'd be away?"

"No, I'm sure that's all. They could have told other people, of course, but I'm not on the society page of the paper. Why would anyone care? I wonder if it would have helped if we'd left Ruffles home." At Higgins's inquiring look, she said, "Our dog. We thought about leaving him home and having Alice come to feed him and walk him every day. Would that have made a difference, if he'd been here to bark?"

"I doubt it, Mrs. Munson. For one thing, there's no guarantee he would have barked. If he knew, or thought he knew, the burglars, he might have let them just walk in."

Mrs. Munson was indignant. "You think friends of ours did this?"

"Someone you know, yes. I wouldn't call them friends. But most of these crimes show inside information. For example, they knew when you'd be out of town and where your jewelry was. That sort of thing. If the thieves don't know you personally, they got information from someone who does. And a couple of times, they've silenced dogs by drugging them. Bank on it: Ruffles was better off at the kennel."

Mrs. Munson shuddered visibly. Alice felt a chill herself. Beside her, Tyler squirmed. She turned toward him and caught him by the arm just as he started for the front door. "Where do you think you're going?"

"Oh, come on, Alice. We're going to be on TV, only all anybody will be able to see is the dumb house."

"That's just too bad. You stay put." Alice let her hair swing forward so she was able to steal a peek at Mrs. Munson without being obvious. At the mention of TV, she had gone rigid. Alice knew how much she must hate this.

"Alice, have you ever known anyone else on

TV with a real robbery?" Tyler was staring out the window again.

"Um-hmm, and I guess they had these same robbers—Mr. Collins and the Olson family." Detective Higgins turned toward her sharply when she said the names, so she looked up and raised her voice slightly to include him. Alice had no idea if this was important to the police or not, but she was willing to help if she could. "I baby-sit sometimes for Mr. Collins's little boy, and the Olsons call me every month when they go to school board meetings. They have a little girl."

"So you know several of the victims, miss." The detective's quiet voice carried clearly. Alice glanced briefly at Tyler, now preoccupied with the TV van's departure. He was safe enough for the moment. She went over to sit beside Mrs. Munson.

"Sure. My dad says I probably know more people than most politicians, I've baby-sat for so many families."

"Alice is a very ambitious young lady, Mr. Higgins. Don't let that quiet, studious look fool you." Mrs. Munson smiled fondly at Alice. "She's been working and saving money for years. She's almost got a monopoly on baby-sitting."

Higgins nodded and sat silently for a moment. He looked at Alice, a peculiar expression on his face, then resumed his questions. "All right, Mrs. Munson. Now, you say you had most of your jewelry with you, but some of it was left here. How much of it is missing, and can you describe it?"

Her surface composure crumbled immediately. "I . . . yes, well. . . ." She took a deep breath and spoke quickly, blinking hard as she spoke. "There wasn't much, and we have a list for the insurance, but my grandmother's necklace and earring set is gone."

"Oh, no!" Alice blurted. "Mrs. Munson, not the pearls? Oh, that's awful." Mrs. Munson blinked back tears.

Alice found Detective Higgins's pale eyes focused on her again. His quiet voice never varied and gave no more clue to his thoughts.

"You know the necklace?"

"It's beautiful. Or, well . . ." she trailed off, then started fresh. "Mrs. Munson showed it to me about a year ago. She had to get it out of a special hiding place. Mrs. Munson, how could thieves have found it?"

"That's part of what we intend to find out," Higgins answered. Alice gave Mrs. Munson's hand a squeeze, then went back to Tyler, who was beginning to get restless. It was bad enough being robbed, Alice thought; she might as well give Mrs. Munson a little privacy.

An hour or so later, Alice got permission to use the kitchen. It felt odd, asking a stranger to let her use a kitchen that was almost as familiar as her own. Nothing had been stolen or damaged in there, except for a shattered sugar bowl. The police were finished taking measurements and photographs, so Alice swept up the sugar before fixing supper for Tyler. Alice went ahead and asked Detective Higgins if he wanted anything. As she expected, he said no.

Tyler picked at his food, and Alice didn't even try to eat anything herself. But she fixed a tray for Mrs. Munson and insisted she eat. Alice hoped the police wouldn't stay much longer; she wasn't sure how much more Mrs. Munson could take. Finally, Detective Higgins stood up.

"Have your husband stop by the station if he can add anything. And we'd appreciate it if you gave us a copy of the insurance report, so we can put everything on the hot list." At Mrs. Munson's blank stare, Detective Higgins explained. "It's a list of stolen goods we circulate to businesses. If some jeweler has an old pearl necklace brought in, he can notify us."

Mrs. Munson nodded vaguely. Alice could

tell that Mrs. Munson wasn't listening; she was just waiting for it to be over. Higgins seemed to realize this as well. With a muttered good night to Alice, he left, taking the last uniformed officer with him.

At the sound of the squad car's doors closing, Mrs. Munson seemed to wake up. She shivered, then sat down on the ruins of the sofa and started crying silently. Alice wasn't sure just when Mr. Munson would be getting there, but she didn't want to leave Mrs. Munson alone. Long after Tyler had fallen into a restless sleep, Alice heard a car pulling into the driveway. Mrs. Munson got to her feet and fled to the door without a word. Alice picked up her books and left as quietly and quickly as possible.

Mr. Munson had half-heartedly offered her a ride home, but she'd refused, knowing he really didn't want to leave. She'd walked the mile home at night more than once before—Anslow wasn't Denver, or even Pueblo. She had called her parents earlier, explaining the situation; they knew she'd be late.

But walking alone—even in peaceful Anslow —was a bit unnerving after the evening she'd spent. The moon was just rising, only a little past new, and the street lights were far apart in this neighborhood. The night was so quiet she could hear her own footsteps, even though she was wearing sneakers. Dogs were barking far away.

Headlights flashed as a car turned down the street. When it honked its horn right behind her, Alice jumped. She whirled around, heart pounding, then recognized the car. It was Steve Ferris—her ex-boyfriend. He still asked her out, refusing to accept that she was with Ryan now. She couldn't avoid Steve entirely, since they sometimes worked at flea markets together, Alice helping her father and Steve scrounging for electronics odds and ends.

Steve called to her, asking if she wanted a lift home. Avoiding him wasn't worth walking alone. Climbing in, she wondered what he was doing in this neighborhood. The question was answered almost at once.

"Hi, Alice. What did the cops find out?" The static noise of a police radio filled the car; Steve had his scanner on. That explained it. The one-way radio monitored the police bands. She knew he often listened to the calls and had learned most of the codes and jargon. He must have heard about the robbery. Still, she was curious.

"How'd you know I'd be walking past here?"

"Cops kept an eye on the Munsons' place

until Mr. Munson got home. I heard them call in when he did, and the station told them to go back on patrol. I figured you'd be walking home, and this is the only sensible route from their place to yours. Simple."

Steve found a lot of things simple. His nondescript looks hid a sharp mind. He pretended to be a nerd, although he didn't fit the stereotype. His looks were more unnoticeable than gawky, he didn't wear thick glasses, he wasn't scrawny. His interest in electronics and radio equipment was really the only part of the role that fit him, and even there Steve approached it in his own way. Alice sometimes thought he used his fingers as an extra brain when he was handling hardware. She loved history and people; resistors and diodes were foreign territory.

"I don't think they really know that much. Mrs. Munson was so upset. I don't blame her; they stole her grandmother's necklace. She was so proud of it."

"Was it worth much?"

"How would I know? I just know she loved it. And they ripped up the couch and smashed all her figurines and souvenirs."

"Those dorky things? I thought you said they were ugly." Steve reached forward and snapped off the scanner. "Want a tape or the radio?"

Alice shook her head. "Neither. It doesn't matter how dumb I thought those figurines were—she loved them. Whoever did it doesn't care anything about people."

Steve cocked his head to one side, as though she'd said something surprising. "I didn't think people who broke into houses and ripped things off were supposed to care about people."

She glared at him. "Okay, so thieves don't care. But I think it's lousy. It doesn't sound like it bothers you much. You've met the Munsons; you ought to care a little more about their feelings!"

"You're a good one to talk about caring about people's feelings." Alice ignored this; he was always trying to start a fight over her breaking up with him. Furious, she thought, *he can't compete with Ryan so he thinks fighting with me will change things.*

The silence grew between them. As they neared her home, Steve broke it. His tone was normal, as though he'd forgotten all about any fights they'd ever had. His unpredictable reactions were part of why she felt she could never figure him out. "Are you going to the Flea Circus on Saturday? Or is your dad?"

The Flea Circus was the flea market they went to most often. "Dad can't, but he wants me to," Alice said. "He finished a necklace last night and he has some new rings. They should sell fairly well. You going?" Flea markets and selling her dad's handmade jewelry made it necessary to ignore Steve's animosity. Once more, she needed a ride.

"The CB's busted. I figure I can find what I need to fix it." His citizens band radio was another piece of equipment, like the scanner, that he'd picked up cheap at a flea market and repaired. Steve pulled up in front of her home. The porch light was on, making his sandy hair look almost white. He looked at her. "Want to go out Saturday night?"

"No." Alice hated it when he did this. She didn't want to ask, but she had no choice. "Will you take me to the Flea Circus, though?"

After a moment he shrugged. "Sure, I'm going anyway. And if you change your mind about Saturday night . . ."

"I won't. Thanks for the ride. Bye." Alice scrambled out of the car in a hurry and almost ran for the house. Behind her, Steve called, "I'll pick you up at eight Saturday morning."

THREE

The next day Alice ate lunch under the trees at the edge of the baseball field. She and her friends always ate there when the weather was decent. Early October was one of her favorite times of year, still warm but no longer hot, with sunny days and clear nights. It was a lot nicer under the trees than in the stuffy cafeteria. The other students scattered around the ball field and bleachers apparently shared her opinion.

Rita and Liz were there ahead of her, since their last class before lunch was right next to the cafeteria. Alice sat down beside them in the grass. As usual, Rita had only a salad. For once, Liz had decided to eat; she actually had a sandwich in addition to her diet soda. Alice sometimes envied Rita her naturally slender figure,

27

but she didn't want to be as thin as Liz. She enjoyed eating too much for that.

"Ryan said they had a burglary last night where you were baby-sitting. How come you didn't just go home?" Rita was lying on her stomach, feet in the air. Her dark eyes were filled with curiosity. As Ryan's twin, she shared his good looks.

"She probably wanted to find out if they had detected anything yet, like, something to do in Anslow," Liz answered. "I've been trying to solve *that* mystery for years." She yawned, feigning elaborate boredom. Liz Hamilton was Rita's best friend. Her parents had a little less money than the Derosas, and Alice thought Liz was a little more snobby to make up for it.

"Knock it off, Liz, I really want to know. Alice, did they ask you questions?" Rita cocked her head to one side, nibbling on a carrot stick.

When Alice started dating Ryan, Rita had adopted her as a friend. The twins were much closer than most brothers and sisters. And it worked both ways; Rita's boyfriend, Eddie, was good friends with Ryan. Alice didn't see her old friends as often as she used to. For one thing, most of them hung around with Steve. The reminders of him were embarrassing.

She nodded. "Yeah, how long I've baby-sat

for them, stuff like that. That wasn't why I stayed, though. I figured Mrs. Munson would need help with Tyler, and I was right. He wanted to get out where the TV guys were."

Liz raised an eyebrow. "And you wouldn't let him? My, aren't you strict. Honestly, Alice, let the brat live a little. You afraid you'll lose some of those precious jobs if a kid acts like a kid for once?"

"At least baby-sitting gives me something to do." Alice tried to keep her voice light. She got tired of Liz's cracks about money-grubbing. "You always say Anslow is the definition of boredom. Maybe you should try it sometime."

Rita abruptly rolled over and sat up. "I can think of something better to do. 'Course, it isn't exactly in Anslow and it isn't making money. It's *spending* it. We've decided it's time for a little run into the city. This weekend. Me, Eddie, Ryan, you. Ryan told me to ask. The guys want to take both cars."

That explained Liz's bad mood, then. Liz resented anyone Ryan dated. Everybody in school knew she wanted to go out with Ryan herself. Everyone except possibly Ryan. If he knew, he'd never shown it.

"Both cars? Uh-oh, I know what that means."

Alice grinned. "The Anslow 500 again. That car of Eddie's belongs on a track someplace."

"Not the car—Eddie." Rita grinned back. "And don't forget the cops. That's part of the game, seeing if the boys can spot all the radar traps."

Eddie and Ryan had played this game before. The first time Alice had been with Ryan, he and Eddie had been racing, and Ryan had gotten stopped for speeding. He'd been more upset about Eddie winning the race than getting the ticket.

"Eddie's gotten a new scanner. And with those two driving," Rita continued with an impish grin, "it won't take long to get to Pueblo. That means more time to shop before dinner."

For a moment, Alice was tempted. With the way she spent money, Rita's shopping expeditions were almost as hair-raising as her twin's driving, but both were fun. Alice was becoming addicted to the excitement. Then she remembered.

"Oh, no. I'd love to go, but I can't. I have to take my dad's jewelry to the flea market. Saturday is the best day for it, and it's my turn again."

Rita shrugged. "Suit yourself, but it's going to be fun."

Alice felt a fresh pang as Eddie and Ryan joined them. Dropping down beside her, Ryan asked, "Rita get it set up for the Saturday?"

Trying to ignore Liz's malicious grin, Alice answered, "Ryan, I can't. You know I have to help my dad. He told me last night he needed me for the weekend."

"That's too bad, Alice." The sympathy in Liz's voice was as artificial as the sweetener in her cola. "What's the name of the place? The Flea Circus? What a dumb name. This weekend you're going to the Flea Circus, and I suppose next weekend you'll hit the Tick Carnival, or maybe the Mosquito Mall, and . . ."

Ryan cut her off. He was looking at Alice and didn't seem to notice the flare of anger in Liz's eyes. "I don't want to go without you, so I'm not." He smiled at Alice. His confidence was infectious, and Alice smiled back at him. Maybe she could get out of the obligation to her dad.

"Ryan, let the junk dealer peddle her junk if she wants to. If she doesn't have sense enough to take shopping with Rita over that, it's her own fault." Unspoken words hung in the air: Liz's offer, *I could go with you.* Eddie was the one who responded.

"Rita can take you next week, Liz. But nobody's going with Rita this time but me. What

31

Ryan and Alice want to do is their business. I didn't hear anyone offering to take *you.*"

Liz glared at Eddie. Rita broke in sharply. "Liz and I have to finish our list for band candy sales, or I'm not going either. The contest for best fall sales ends next week, and any contest I'm in, I win."

Ryan hauled Alice to her feet and pulled her off to one side, as the conversation shifted to candy sales. Alice thought it was funny, the way Liz and Rita laughed at baby-sitting and flea markets, when they spent so much time selling stuff for the school band. Of course, Rita was famous for being highly competitive.

Ryan and Alice stood between a pair of trees. It wasn't true privacy, but they were almost out of earshot and the trees provided some shielding. Ryan combed Alice's long hair back from her face with his fingers.

"No hiding behind the hair, Alice." He continued stroking the blond strands. "Now. Look at me and tell me you don't want to go Saturday."

"Ryan, that's not fair. You know I want to go, but wanting to and being able to aren't the same thing. I can ask my dad, but if he says no, that's it."

He dropped his hand from her hair. "I

couldn't take you out to celebrate yesterday, I can't take you out on Saturday—look, are we going together or not?"

Alice searched his eyes anxiously. "Ryan, of course we're going together. I can't help it if I'm stuck this weekend, but I'm not stuck on Friday. We could go out then." That was a little white lie, since she had a job lined up with the Raineys, but she wasn't going to worry about that now.

It worked. Ryan smiled, and Alice relaxed as he began combing her hair with his fingers again. "All right. Ask your dad about Saturday, though. If I can get a double helping of you, I want it. Stuck working tonight, I suppose?"

"Not till eight-thirty. We could do something first." The bell rang in the distance, and they started back toward the building. Ahead of them, Eddie had one arm around Rita's waist and the other around Liz's; the bickering must have stopped. Alice was wondering how she could get out of her job on Friday. This time Ryan was going to come first.

That evening, Alice arrived at the Larkins' a little early, hoping to catch up on her homework. She hadn't been able to cancel the job for Friday, but she could do that the next morning. Saturday she was going to be at the flea market

—her father had been impatient when she asked if she could skip. They needed some jewelry sales, and her parents had made plans to go out of town for the weekend.

"Your mother and I haven't seen the Bordens in two years. Now, if a date with Ryan, who you see every day, is really all that important, I guess we can miss seeing Phil and Pat for another two years while you have a social life. . . ." Her father's sarcasm was a bit heavy-handed at times.

The Larkins weren't regulars; Alice hadn't seen them in at least two months. The first thing she noticed when she went in was a new carpet in the living room. Alice thought it was a big improvement from the old one. She phrased it more politely than that when she complimented Mrs. Larkin on it.

"I didn't want to get it." Mrs. Larkin's lips were pressed tightly together. "Never mind that now. I've got the police and fire numbers taped on top of the phone, and here's a list of places you can call if you need to reach me. I'll be at this first number for about an hour, then I'll be at one of the others. Try them both if you need to."

Alice took the list, wondering when Mrs. Larkin had become such a worrier. She was usually vague about where they'd be and had never bothered leaving a number before. Now she acted as if she were a new mother, leaving her baby for the first time. "Is something wrong? Are you expecting a phone call or anything?" Alice asked.

"No, nothing wrong except criminals in Anslow." The tight lips were back. "Be sure to fasten the bolt after I'm out."

The heavy door looked new, and the deadbolt lock certainly was. "Are you afraid of burglars? We'll be all right, honest."

Mrs. Larkin took a deep breath. "I suppose it's foolish of me to worry about it now. It's not as though they're likely to come just to ruin the new rug. Sorry, Alice; I guess this is what they mean about locking the barn door after the horse is stolen. We were robbed six weeks ago."

"What? Oh, I'm so sorry. I had no idea." Alice was appalled. "They ruined the old rug?"

"It looked like they poured motor oil and ink on it. I don't know; I just took it to the dump. I think we were the first robbery. We thought it was just kids, getting into trouble."

Alice felt her stomach tighten, the way it did when she watched a scary movie. She vaguely remembered hearing about a burglary back then, but she hadn't paid much attention to it.

That had been around the time Ryan had first shown an interest in her. Between the excitement of being a senior, and Ryan, Alice hadn't been paying much attention to news.

This made two nights in a row she'd come in contact indirectly with the break-in artists. She shivered and hoped the next encounter wouldn't be in her own home. Or while she was baby-sitting. After Mrs. Larkin left, Alice fastened the deadbolt with as much care as though an entire street gang was just outside.

This was one of the easy sitting jobs. The two Larkin children were very young and already asleep. Alice checked on them briefly, then sat down with her homework and got busy. By eleven o'clock, she had everything done except for the last section of math. She turned on the TV to catch the late news. If she didn't quite finish the math tonight, no harm done; she had study hall right before class the next day.

The top news story was still the Munson burglary. Alice turned up the sound.

". . . an escalating series of incidents. So far, the criminals haven't broken into an occupied home, but police fear it's just a matter of time before that happens. A police spokesperson said that homeowners should check the locks on all their doors and replace them if needed. Earlier break-ins thought to be related to the Munson burglary include . . ." A series of stills of houses flashed across the screen, each with a name in block capitals across the bottom.

Alice got up and went to check the dead bolt once again. For the first time in all her years of sitting, Alice was nervous about being alone in a house. Something bothered her about the newscast, but she couldn't think of what it was. If the police were hoping to scare people into locking up, they were succeeding nicely. Alice checked the front door as well, then went back to see what was on the late movie. The words of one of the Munsons' neighbors, interviewed on the news, echoed in her head: "We're starting to be afraid in our own homes." Alice could sympathize.

As she turned on an old sit-com, Alice suddenly realized what had been bothering her about the news story. Every one of the break-in victims listed was someone she knew.

In fact, they were all baby-sitting clients of hers.

FOUR

By Friday evening, Alice was more than ready for a night out with Ryan. The week had been one aggravation after another. She had been tense baby-sitting alone at night, and at school, Liz had kept up a steady barrage of needling remarks about junk dealers. Alice was glad when Rita and Liz skipped lunch on Thursday and Friday, at Rita's insistence, to work on candy sales. Without Liz around, lunch with Ryan became the bright spot in Alice's otherwise dreary days.

She still hadn't been able to reach Mrs. Rainey by phone to cancel. So that afternoon, Alice stopped there on her way home from school. Mrs. Rainey was upset by the last-minute cancellation, and Alice felt a little guilty, but only a little. Mrs. Rainey wasn't a regular, preferring to take her son with her whenever she could. At two and a half, he was energetic and noisy, but Mrs. Rainey believed kids belonged in public as much as in private. Lack of a sitter was less of a handicap to her than to most parents.

Alice's parents were almost ready to leave for the weekend when she got home. She was glad she wasn't going with them. The Bordens were nice, and their ranch was beautiful, but she would have been the youngest person present by a quarter of a century. Her folks would have more fun without her, and she wouldn't be bored on her own. She ate a hasty snack with them, helped her mom finish packing a suitcase, and waved a thankful good-bye.

The house hers, she went upstairs to get ready for her date. Alice hadn't gone for the standard frills in her room, but there were *Alice in Wonderland* touches here and there. Reproductions of the Tenniel illustrations from the books shared the walls with travel posters from around the world and a few college pennants of schools she was interested in. Books crowded the shelves and the desk, and more were piled untidily on the floor near her bed. The blues in the bedspread and curtains matched her eyes.

She didn't know if Ryan was planning on having the celebration they'd missed earlier in the week, which posed a problem. Should she should dress up or go casual? Ryan would be there by seven-thirty, and it was already a few minutes past six-thirty. So much for her plans for a nice leisurely bubble bath. She headed for the bathroom to take a shower instead.

When she came out, toweling her hair, she glanced at the clock and was horrified. Five after seven! She grabbed the dryer and started getting her hair dry enough for a French braid, while looking over the clothes in her closet. Finally she decided on her favorite jeans, with a white crop-top and her new light purple shirt over it, tied at the waist. The shirt had come from her last shopping trip with Rita, the only thing she had dared buy. With low heels and some jewelry, she would look dressy enough for most things, while being casual enough for anything. Her hair dry, Alice dressed quickly, then started braiding.

By the time she was ready, it was seven-forty. Alice let out her breath in a long whoosh. Ryan's chronic lateness had let her off the hook once more. Downstairs, she sat in the big chair by the front window in the living room and started reading, glancing out the window occasionally at the sound of a passing car.

The book was a new novel by one of her favorite authors, and for a while Alice lost track of the time. Finally, she marked her page and glanced at the clock. With a start, she realized that almost an hour had passed. Ryan had been late before, in fact he was almost always late, but it was now well past eight-thirty.

She went back to the big chair and flopped down in it. This time, she just stared out the window. Minutes passed slowly. The street the Flemings lived on dead-ended, so there wasn't much traffic besides the neighborhood residents. After checking her watch for the eighth time in five minutes, Alice got up again, exasperated. No cars had gone by, and she couldn't think of a more boring way to spend Friday night. She didn't want to finish her book. She turned on the TV, but couldn't really find anything she was interested in watching. After channel-hopping for a while, she gave up. She really wasn't in the mood for TV anyway. The radio wasn't any better as a distraction. It cheerfully informed her there were only five more minutes till headline news coverage, then they'd be back with the hottest rock in town.

She ignored the commercial. Five minutes till nine.

She got up, sat back down, stared out the window, changed radio stations. She kept coming back to the front window, watching for Ryan's car, beginning to get worried. Maybe he'd been in an accident? Her hand stretched toward the telephone several times, but it would look silly if she'd just gotten the times mixed up, or if—or if—that was the problem. She couldn't think of very many harmless things that would make him this late without calling. Just bad ones, such as breakdowns and accidents and tickets.

Just as she made up her mind to call, the phone rang. Alice snatched it up, ready to be angry as soon as she knew he was all right. But it wasn't Ryan.

"Alice? It's Steve. Since you aren't working tonight, I thought I'd come over. All right?"

Alice took a tighter grip on the phone and looked at her watch yet again. Nine-fifteen! And now Steve was tying up the line, which meant this was probably the exact moment Ryan would try to call.

"No, it is *not* all right! I happen to have a date." *If he ever gets here.* She ignored the internal dialogue and went on. "I do a few things besides baby-sitting, you know."

"Yeah." Steve's voice was a little flat, as though there were a lot he wasn't saying. "All with Ryan. I just wanted to talk to you for a while, that's all."

"Well, I can't right now." Not that she wanted to. "Anyway, it's insulting, calling this late on a Friday night for a date."

"I didn't say this was a date; I said I wanted to talk."

"Steve, you can talk to me in the morning when we go to the Flea Circus. Whatever it is, it can wait, can't it?"

"I suppose it'll have to. I just thought, since you weren't working—okay, okay, I'll see you tomorrow at eight."

"Wait a minute, Steve. Just how did you know that I wasn't sitting? I canceled this afternoon. How would you know when I'm working and when I'm not working, Steve Ferris? And just what business is it of yours, anyway?"

"Tell you in the morning. Have fun with Richie Rich."

Alice crashed the receiver back down on the cradle. She had dated Steve for over a year, and while they'd gotten along okay, it had never really been a passionate romance. But now he was almost chasing her, acting more interested in her than when they'd been dating. Maybe he just couldn't stand the thought of losing her to Ryan. But Alice didn't like the idea of being spied on, and she couldn't think of any way that Steve had known her baby-sitting schedule.

Come to think of it, he'd been acting peculiar for a couple of weeks. More than ever, Alice regretted her dad's insistence on the flea market. The idea of spending a large part of Saturday with Steve and his active hostility was less than appealing.

She stood there, wondering what had gotten into Steve and how she was going to survive an entire day with him, when the doorbell brought her back to awareness of the time. She hurried to the front door, glancing at the hall clock as she passed. Nine twenty-five; it had better be Ryan.

It was. He stepped in with a muttered "Hi," and went into the living room. Usually his expression was pleasant, even when he was upset. It wasn't now; he was scowling. Alice waited for a tale of disaster to explain the delay and Ryan's expression. When he just sat down without a word, her own anger crept up again. If there was a good reason for being two hours late, now was the time for him to give it.

"Ryan? What's wrong? Why didn't you call?" He stared at her with a look on his face that Alice couldn't understand. His dark brown eyes searched her face for a moment, then looked away. A little of the tension left his body, and he leaned back on the couch.

"Rita. She and Eddie had a bad fight, and Rita was pretty upset. I didn't want to leave until they settled down."

"You could have called." The flat statement was all Alice trusted herself to say.

"Look, I'm sorry, I just didn't think about it, okay? They were both yelling, and Rita was crying, and I lost my head a little."

Alice took a deep breath. "I don't care if you *were* born seventeen minutes ahead of Rita. I think she can handle her love life on her own without big brother."

"In case you've forgotten, Eddie is my best friend. I don't like it when my kid sister and my best friend are yelling at each other. Look, are we going out or are we going to stand here fighting?"

Alice reached for her purse. "Fine. Let's go." Her anger eased a bit. It was obvious he wasn't telling her the entire story, but something had really rocked him. She'd give him a little time to sort it out on his own.

Once they were on the road, Ryan's driving was even wilder than usual. As they fishtailed on the turn out of town, Alice gritted her teeth. Once they were on the main highway, however, he let their speed drop back down to the limit.

"I should have said this before—you look great tonight. I like that shirt."

"Rita helped me pick it out," Alice said, relaxing as he did. "Where are we going anyway?" It was too late for a trip into Pueblo, and the last movie at the only theater in Anslow would be almost out.

"Just out to the lake for a while. I'm really sorry, Alice. I was going to take you out for that celebration, but I'm just not up for it. I hope you ate something."

"It's cool. I ate with my folks before they left. It's just as well we aren't going clear into the city; I still have the Flea Circus in the morning. I can't sleep in."

"Wish you weren't stuck with that. We could have made up for tonight. It's half gone already." He turned onto the gravel road leading out to the small lake.

Ryan pulled around the loop at the end of the road and parked on the gravel above the path that led down to the lake. On summer afternoons, the entire area was jammed with cars, since half the town's population spent as much time at the lake as possible. The people who came to the lake at this time of night though weren't interested in swimming. Alice could see another car parked on the far side of the turn-around, but local custom treated all cars parked by the lake after dark as invisible. Ryan turned the radio on and put his arm around her.

Alice leaned against him, but she resented his assumption that she would be willing to make out, as though nothing had happened. Before he kissed her, she asked, "Ryan? Why didn't you just let Rita and Eddie handle it?"

The inside of the car was almost completely dark. The moon was less than a quarter full and there was only one street light, on the other side of the parking area. But even in the dim light, she could see Ryan's jaw muscles tighten as he pulled back.

"Let Rita and Eddie handle what? You mean the fight?"

"Well, how serious could it have been? And even if it was, can't Rita make up her own mind about boyfriends? If she doesn't want to go out with Eddie anymore, that's her decision."

"You don't know anything about it." His voice was half-choked with anger. "I just don't like them fighting. Not like that. Sometimes you don't really know what people are like until they're upset."

Alice knew Rita could have quite a temper, and she said so. "And she's been talking about going to school back east next year, anyway. You won't be able to protect her from her own temper then."

"Just get off my case, Alice, will you? I'm sorry I didn't call, but you keep this up and I won't be calling anymore at all. For anything."

Alice had been looking forward to this evening for most of the week. Now it was turning out to be a complete disaster. She and Ryan had never had a fight before; he'd never been mean. Why was everything going wrong since she'd heard about the scholarship?

"I didn't mean to give you a hard time Ryan, but I got worried when you were so late. I was afraid you'd had a wreck or gotten yourself arrested for speeding or something."

He laughed. "Never happen, babe. I can outrun 'em all, you know that. And I'm too good a driver to wipe out."

She let out a shaky laugh herself. "Yeah, but you don't have to keep proving it to me! You know, this is all so stupid. Think about it— we're fighting over another couple's fight!"

"You're right, that's pretty stupid." Once

more, Ryan pulled her over to him. "I can think of a whole lot better things to do."

As he kissed her, the evening started to right itself. At the back of Alice's mind, she couldn't help feeling some resentment toward Rita and Eddie for almost ruining her evening.

Finally, she pulled back, slightly dizzy. She always stayed in control; she wasn't ready to handle anything heavier. Staying calm hadn't been a problem with Steve, but with Ryan everything was so intense. He was nuzzling her neck now, his breath hot against her skin.

The other car started with a roar that made them both jump. It echoed over the lake, unnaturally loud in the night quiet. Alice took advantage of the break to lean forward and fiddle with the radio. As she turned the knob, the reception improved suddenly. It was much later than she'd realized; the midnight news wrap-up was on. She was about to turn it off when a familiar name caught her ear.

"Turning to local news, Mr. and Mrs. Charles Rainey appear to be the latest victims in the ongoing crime spree in Anslow. On their arrival home earlier this evening, they discovered their home had been ransacked and robbed. In a new twist on these burglaries, the baby-sitter, sixteen-year-old Nancy Ettinger, was found to be missing. A police spokesperson refused to speculate on the possibility that Ms. Ettinger might be involved, while her parents expressed concern. . . ."

FIVE

The alarm went off at seven. Alice rolled over and tried to ignore it, but its shrill insistence continued. At last she roused enough to turn it off. She wanted to go back to sleep, but Steve would be picking her up soon for the flea market. It would be just like him to show up early. She wondered what his call the night before had been about. She used to think she understood him, but these days he made less sense to her than his electronics.

Her head ached and there was a sour taste in her mouth. She had awakened several times during the night with bad dreams. All Alice could recall about the nightmares was a sense of terror and something pursuing her. Vague dreams were sometimes the most terrifying ones.

A shower took care of most of the headache but it didn't improve her mood any. The night before had ended the way it began—in disaster. After hearing the news about the burglary, she'd made Ryan drive her home. She hadn't explained why, and the fight had started all over again. By the time he dropped her off, they weren't even speaking.

She turned the fight over in her mind. She wasn't sure if she was ready to think of anything long-term. For years, her plan had been college first, then men. Ryan had changed things. When he was around, she didn't take things quite so seriously. She had fun. And it might be more than just a good time. She wasn't sure, but she wanted to find out.

She should have told him what was bothering her, but it was too hard to explain. It felt as though she were somehow involved; as though she was at the center of whatever was happening in Anslow. Her feelings weren't logical, she knew, but she couldn't shake them. She knew how dumb it would sound to Ryan. So instead, she'd wound up fighting with him, and had nightmares all night and a throbbing head in the morning. Great, just great.

She pulled on an old pair of jeans and a

T-shirt and redid the French braid. Then she went downstairs and got out the special leather case her father had bought to display his jewelry. She opened it, double-checking that she had everything she needed. The new azurite necklaces and the onyx and silver rings were all in place. She added the turquoise pavé ring he'd finished on Thursday. Now she was ready.

There was time to sit down with coffee and the newspaper. These crimes were the biggest story the *Anslow Answer* had covered since a local county supervisor had been caught taking kickbacks from the company that sold office supplies to the county. That had been good for circulation and made a nice political scandal, but it wasn't as good as a serial crime. The *Answer* was making the most of it.

The burglary at the Raineys' took up most of the front page. Alice read every word. According to the paper, Nancy Ettinger had been a last-minute substitute for the regular sitter. Alice's skin crawled as she realized *she* was the "regular sitter." When the Raineys had gotten home at nine, they had found the door wide open and a smashed window at the back. The Raineys' child was safely asleep in his own bed, but Nancy Ettinger had been missing.

A sidebar on the story gave a description of Nancy, with comments from people who knew her. Everyone said they didn't believe she'd do anything bad. From what Alice remembered, she didn't think so either. Nancy wasn't in any of her classes, but she recognized the photo at the top of the column. It was a school picture, showing a girl with short curly hair and a wide grin. At the bottom, her tearful mother was pictured standing next to Detective Higgins.

The stories continued on the inside pages. Alice skipped the continuation on page thirteen, which summarized every crime to date. None of it meant anything to her, or explained why she felt as though it should mean something. Finally, with a sigh, she turned to the comics.

After she finished reading her favorites, she glanced at the clock. It was a few minutes after eight. Instead of being early, Steve was late. After another ten minutes had passed, Alice felt a flash of irritation. She was getting tired of waiting for men. She wondered how long it would be before she could afford a car. Possibly the scholarship money would stretch far enough so she could get a clunker. But that didn't help now. Location was everything at the Flea Circus; if Steve didn't hurry up, all the best places would be taken.

Finally she heard his old Plymouth pulling into the driveway. She grabbed the leather case and her knapsack and ran out the side door, slamming it behind her. She slung the case in the back seat and started to climb in, but Steve stopped her.

"Just a second, Alice. Before we go anywhere, there's something we've got to talk about. Let's go inside."

"What? Steve, are you crazy? Look at the time; half the best places are probably already gone. I'll talk about whatever you want, but let's do it on the way, huh? I promised Dad."

Steve just sat there. Obviously, he wasn't going to start the car. Exasperated, Alice yanked the case out of the car. Almost stomping, she headed back to the door. The fastest way to get going was to humor him. As a final straw, her key stuck. She wrestled with the lock for a couple of minutes. It finally opened and they went in.

She set the case down just inside the door as Steve went through the kitchen into the living room. Alice followed him and remained standing. Whatever this was about, she wasn't going to give him a chance to make them any later. If he wanted to rake up the past, or start harassing her about Ryan again, she'd walk out.

When Steve started speaking, she almost did walk out. His first words seemed so irrelevant. "Why didn't you baby-sit for the Raineys last night?"

"Steve, you've finally lost it completely. I don't know why you think it's any of your business where I go or what I do, but I don't like being spied on, and if you don't stop . . ."

"I haven't been spying on you." There was no apology in his voice. "But a lot of people are going to want the answer to that question."

As she opened her mouth for a furious reply, he continued, "They found Nancy Ettinger. She's dead."

For a few seconds Alice's mind refused to understand his words. They made no sense; there was no connection with what they'd been talking about, no connection with her. She tried to speak twice before her voice worked.

"Dead?" Her voice was no more than a croak, and she swallowed to loosen the sudden tightness. She found herself sitting in the big chair and realized her knees had decided not to hold her up any longer. "Nancy is dead? You mean the burglars . . . do the police think . . . Steve, what happened!"

"Yeah, the police think. Alice, it was murder."

She sat there, unable to make a sound as he went on.

"They were pretty suspicious last night. If she'd been part of the gang doing this, there wouldn't have been any reason for her to be missing. If she'd been letting them in places, the cops would have caught her a long time before now. They started searching this morning. The dogs from the Highway Patrol went straight from the house to the irrigation ditch."

The ditch. When it was in use, the fast-running water was a deadly temptation for toddlers. Even when it was dry, kids had been known to fall into it. It ran along the back of the Raineys' property. Her mind seized on it, trying to avoid hearing what she knew was coming.

"Nancy was in it, covered up with brush. Her head was smashed in."

Alice closed her eyes. When the sound of Steve's voice stopped, she opened them, to find him staring at her.

"Are you okay?"

She nodded, barely moving her head. After another searching look, he went on. "The cops got pretty gabby on the radio about it. I think this is the first murder they've had in years.

They found a crowbar next to the body. There's blood and stuff on it, but no fingerprints."

Alice found her voice again, although it sounded too loud in her own ears. "Are they sure it was the same thieves who broke into the other places? Why would they kill Nancy? All they've ever done is steal stuff, or break it! I mean, I can't believe anyone in Anslow gets off on killing people!"

"The police think it was an accident. Most of the lights were out, and she had some videos from the rental place. The phone was smashed in the family room. They figure she was watching the video and the crooks thought the house was empty. They broke in, and she tried to call for help. Whoever it was tried to stop her."

"They did stop her." The words were a whisper.

"Yeah. They did. Like I said, they figure whoever it was didn't mean to kill her, just to shut her up. After she was dead it looks like they just threw some things around and grabbed stuff to make it look like a burglary, then lugged her out to the ditch and piled brush over her." Steve had been talking as though he were on one of the true-crime shows, all tough and professional, but his voice faltered at the end. He took a deep breath and concluded, "Even if they didn't mean to kill her, the cops are still calling it murder."

Alice shivered. She hadn't really known Nancy, but she was a student at Anslow Union High, just as Alice was. Or she had been a student. Now she was a murder victim.

A thought struck Alice, and she spoke without thinking. "Thank God I was out with Ryan." Steve scowled, but she hardly noticed. "That could have been me! I was supposed to have sat for the Raineys. I mean, if I hadn't canceled to go out with Ryan, I might have been there and . . ." Her voice trailed away.

"Yeah, I know you canceled. I still want to know why."

Suddenly, Alice's fear was overpowered by a jolt of anger. "It's none of your business! Do you keep tabs on me all the time, are you following me around town or something? I still want to know how you know so much about *my* schedule!"

She stopped abruptly as his face filled with a matching rage. Before he could say anything, the doorbell rang. Fighting for self-control, Alice strode over and opened it. Detective Higgins was standing in the doorway. An officer in uniform stood behind him, and there was a squad car parked at the curb. She hadn't heard them pull up.

"Ms. Fleming? I wonder if we could ask you a few questions."

SIX

"Questions?" Alice repeated blankly. Why would the police want to question her? Then she realized Mrs. Rainey would have told them about her canceling. She stepped back. "Please, come in."

She motioned them to the couch. Steve had moved over to the chair at her dad's desk, against the far wall. It was littered with odds and ends, overflow from his jewelry making. Steve sat there fiddling with some stones and scraps of gold wire, not introducing himself or offering to leave. Detective Higgins stared at him for a moment, then sat down. Alice had the feeling that Steve's face had gone into a file in Higgins's head. She sat down and asked how she could help him.

Higgins looked around. "Are your parents home?"

"No, they're out of town for the weekend."

He hesitated for a moment. Then he asked, "Ms. Fleming, how old are you?"

Bewildered, Alice said, "Seventeen. I'll be eighteen next March. What does that have to do with anything?"

Higgins didn't answer, but he was clearly bothered by her answer. He exchanged glances with the uniformed man. "You may prefer to wait for your parents, miss. Or a lawyer. You're under no obligation to answer questions if you choose not to."

She shook her head, a little impatient. "Why on earth would I want a lawyer? Go ahead, ask the questions."

At a slight nod from Higgins, the uniformed officer got out a notebook and pen. The detective started with a question Alice was already sick of hearing. "First, why did you cancel your appointment to baby-sit for the Raineys last night?"

Alice hadn't answered Steve, but the police were different. "I had a date. Mrs. Rainey asked me to sit last week, but then on Wednesday my boyfriend asked me to go out. I decided I'd rather go out."

"Him?" Higgins indicated Steve with a jerk of his head. Steve didn't react, either to the question or to the attention.

"No, not him." Alice was exasperated; she couldn't get away from Steve. "Ryan. Ryan Derosa." Higgins's eyes flicked to his partner at the name Derosa, then he indicated Steve with a nod.

"And he is?"

"Steve Ferris. He's just a friend." She didn't feel very friendly toward Steve, but saying that was easier than explaining the actual relationship.

"So Ryan Derosa asked you for a date on Wednesday. According to Mrs. Rainey, you didn't cancel the sitting job until late Friday afternoon. Why?"

"I couldn't get hold of her earlier. Either her phone was busy or she was out. I stopped on my way home from school Friday." Alice felt a mixture of guilt and gratitude at her narrow escape. "I usually try to give more warning if I cancel, and I don't cancel often, but it just worked out that way. It was an important date."

"An important date? Where did you go? What was so important about it?"

"Well . . ." Alice stopped. It was impossible to describe the tension and the missed celebration to a police detective. "As it turned out, we just went out to the lake." She ducked her head, letting her hair swing forward to conceal the blush she felt creeping over her face. Going to the lake at night had only one meaning in Anslow.

She was expecting more questions about the date and wished that Steve would leave. The next question caught her off guard.

"What did you expect Mrs. Rainey to do, left without a sitter less than an hour before she was supposed to leave? She told us you knew their plans; in fact she was getting ready to drive in and meet her husband in Pueblo when you came by. She was upset, and you knew it."

Were the police scolding her for letting Mrs. Rainey down? "She takes Charles with her most of the time anyway. She says kids are portable. I didn't really think about it, but I guess I just assumed she'd take him."

"In other words, you had good reason to believe the house would be empty. Is that correct?"

They thought she was one of the burglars! Despite her own vague fear about the crimes, she hadn't thought of herself as a suspect. She had felt more like the target.

"What do you mean?" Her voice was shrill

and she fought to bring it under control. When she spoke again, it was with only an occasional tremor to mark her distress. "I could have been lying there dead myself. Why would I be part of it?"

"We haven't said you are, Ms. Fleming," Higgins said in his quiet voice. Alice was beginning to see how his method worked. He never raised his voice, never spoke quickly, never showed his feelings. He just said what he needed to and watched your reaction.

"I'm sorry. No, you haven't accused me directly, but I can add things up. You must think I'm involved. But I could just as easily have been the victim, couldn't I?" She nodded at Steve. "He heard this morning that Nancy had been found." *Dead.*

"If you weren't involved in the earlier crimes, if you had been there alone, and *if* the break-in had occurred in the same fashion, then yes. You could have been injured. Right now we're just checking possibilities. You had reason to believe the Raineys' house would be empty?"

"I didn't think about it either way," she said tiredly. If he thought she was interested in empty houses, she wouldn't change his mind by arguing.

"Where were you between five P.M. and seven P.M. last night, Ms. Fleming?"

"I told you, I had a date."

"Yes, so you said. With Ryan Derosa. What time did Mr. Derosa arrive here, and where did you go? Just the lake? If you were just going to the lake, why was the date so important?"

"I thought we were going someplace else, but Ryan was late. He got tied up and he didn't get here till nine-thirty."

"Who was with you between five and nine, Ms. Fleming?"

"Well, my folks didn't leave here till almost six, I guess, then I got ready, and I read, and . . ." She stopped, upset at the sight of the uniformed man carefully writing down her words.

Higgins persisted, his voice unvarying. "And? Did you go anyplace, see anyone, *call* anyone? Can anyone say for certain that you were here during that time?"

"Steve called." Now the memory of that maddening phone call came as a relief. She turned toward him, but his face was as carefully expressionless as Higgins. "Steve, you called."

"I called at nine-fifteen. The Raineys got home at nine-ten. I heard the call to the squad car on my scanner."

Alice still wondered why she was a suspect. She asked Higgins, putting it just that bluntly. His answer chilled her.

"Each crime in this case has been a little more reckless, a little more violent. We were afraid someone would get hurt before the end, although we didn't expect this. But we've checked the profiles of every break-in we know about. After the first one, we can't pin times closely enough to do any good, and the victims are scattered all over town. In fact, we've only been able to find one factor in common. You, Ms. Fleming."

Steve dropped the large hunk of petrified wood her dad used as a paperweight. The thud stopped all speech for a moment. His face as red as Alice's had been, he bent to pick it up with a muttered apology. Higgins ignored Steve and continued.

"You're the connecting link, Ms. Fleming. Every one of the victims used you at one time or another as a baby-sitter. In addition, each case has involved some sort of insider information. Location of items that were stolen, schedules, hidden spare keys—when will people stop thinking they can hide those things, for God's sake?—anyway, there's been something. Something that you've been in a position to know. In some cases the victims have told us that you knew the information involved. So, I think it's about time you started giving me some facts instead of asking more questions."

"But I don't know anything!" Alice suddenly remembered one of the bad dreams she'd had. She'd been trapped in a small room, and the door had vanished into smooth wall, leaving no way out. She had the same feeling now. The dream was better; at least it ended when she woke up.

"You may not have committed the actual burglaries yourself. There were a few indications at least one strong male was involved." His eyes moved to Steve, who sat as frozen as the stone he still held. "Maybe you passed along information without realizing the use it was being put to. But there's a limit to the size of coincidence I'm ready to swallow. All of those people just happening to be clients of yours, all of that information you just happened to know—that's over the limit."

The rest of the questioning went past Alice in a blur. Details of when she had baby-sat for whom, what schedules she had known, who kept which items where. She answered mostly in monosyllables, numbness blanketing her mind. Several times, Higgins interrupted to ask if she wanted to wait for her parents, or a lawyer. She shook her head; she just wanted to get it over with. She did notice Higgins seemed to know all about her scholarship hopes and college plans. Any good this did her as a character reference was lost in the motive it provided. Someone had been telling Higgins a lot about her. She remembered Mrs. Munson, answering questions that day: ". . . been working and saving money for years . . . almost got a monopoly on baby-sitting." And no doubt all of the others as well. All of her clients, her friends. They'd encouraged her and been almost as proud of her as her parents.

Her parents. Alice's stomach contracted into a tight ball thinking of them. How would she ever tell them about being a suspect in a murder? She awakened to the fact that Higgins had said something and was waiting for a response. He repeated it.

"I said, Ms. Fleming, you're not under arrest, but we'd prefer it if you didn't leave this jurisdiction for a while. If your family hasn't got a lawyer, perhaps your parents should consider consulting one. If you decide to tell us anything, you have our number." He held out his hand and, automatically, she took the small card he offered. She glanced down at it: Detective

Art Higgins, Anslow Police, a phone number. He made his way to the door, followed by the man in uniform. The uniformed officer hadn't said a word the entire time, just sat there taking notes.

Alice leaned her forehead against the cool, smooth wood of the door. They were gone. Now the nightmare would be over and she could wake up. She didn't. Like it or not, she was already awake.

"You couldn't have been that surprised." Steve's voice startled her. She turned, to find him standing right behind her. "I thought they'd say something last week, after the Munsons were hit."

She shook her head slightly, still numb. She found her voice. "Why? You expected this?"

He scowled. His features were regular to the point of being bland, but they reflected emotions graphically when he allowed them to. "C'mon. You telling me you didn't spot all those clients of yours?"

"Of course I didn't! I haven't really been following it that much. I didn't even know the Larkins had been robbed till I was there the other night."

"It was in the paper; I remember the article. How come you didn't see it?"

"I don't know. I'd been busy with Senior Startup." The combination open house and kickoff dance for incoming seniors had been the first time she'd really met Ryan. "I was too excited over school." And Ryan.

He turned back into the room, speaking over his shoulder. "Were you at that thing? That's the only one they can pin a time on. It sounds as if you have an alibi for it, at least."

"Not really. I almost missed it. I was working that afternoon. By the time I went over there, there was less than half an hour left." Time enough to meet Ryan, not time enough for an alibi.

Steve bent down at the end of the couch, rummaging in the peach basket they used for old newspapers. He came up with the first section of that day's paper. It wasn't even ten o'clock, but it felt as though the paper should be yellowing with age. So much had happened since she'd read about what she thought was just another robbery. She saw the photo of Nancy on the side column and shuddered.

Steve turned past the first page to the continuation she'd skipped. There was a long column filled with fine print, summarizing all the crimes. He held out the paper in a wordless invitation. She moved alongside him reluctantly. His finger traced down the column, stabbing at each boldface name. It could have been the roster from her baby-sitting diary, the special notebook where she kept track of all her jobs and the individual quirks of each client. Some of the names were regulars, some were people she'd only seen once or twice, but they were all in the book.

Steve didn't say anything, just pointed to name after name. As he reached the bottom of the page and folded the paper back up, she started to shake. She bit her lip, her standard way of controlling tears. This time, though, it didn't work. Her control and her nerves had been stretched too far. The tears spilled down her cheeks.

Steve's arm slid around her shoulders. It felt familiar there. She forgot their recent fights and buried her face in his chest. She'd known Steve all her life; she'd dated him for over a year. He was her friend. Right now, that was what she needed. She stopped fighting for control and let go, soaking the front of Steve's shirt. He tightened his arms around her.

She didn't notice when his embrace changed, from comfort to something else. When the first wave of tears had passed, leaving her spent, she felt his lips touching the top of her head lightly.

74

His hand was stroking her hair and he was murmuring something. She pulled back abruptly, paying no attention to the small part of her mind that wanted to go on. That was just habit, from when she and Steve had been dating.

"No, Steve. Thanks for the hug, I needed it, but no more, please." She fished in her pockets for a ratty Kleenex. "I'm a mess. I wished you'd gotten here sooner; we would have been on the road before they got here."

His hand started to reach for her, then pulled back as he resumed his no-expression expression. "I was waiting for them."

"What?"

"On the scanner. It's easy to tell what the cops are up to, once you learn the jargon and some of their codes."

Which meant he had let her in for the whole ordeal. It would have happened sooner or later, but she would have preferred later. Why hadn't he warned her?

"Why didn't you *say* something! You knew they were coming and you just kept asking me about baby-sitting. . . ."

"Yeah. Same question they asked. You never did answer me, and you didn't do much better with them."

"What business is it of yours! *I* asked *you* that

before they got here, and I notice you never answered me either!"

His eyes blazing, Steve grabbed both her shoulders in his hands. His fingers dug in painfully. "I don't know if you noticed it, but Higgins seems to think there's some connection between us. I used to think there was, until you started liking your snooty rich friends better. But somebody's been feeding the cops a line about the two of us. You heard that bit about at least one guy being involved. I don't have an alibi for the night of the first robbery, and they know it. From what I've heard on the scanner, I think they suspect me too."

"Well, should they?" Alice's eyes blazed back at him. Steve shook her a little, then dropped his hands. "I didn't even know all those people had been robbed. You know a lot more about it than I do!"

"So you say." He turned toward the door. "The question is, do I believe you? Bye, Alice."

SEVEN

Alice's parents arrived home late that afternoon. She had called them after Steve left, but she hadn't given them the entire story. Just telling them the police had come by to ask questions was bad enough. Her father asked why she had agreed to talk to the police without her parents there, and had snorted in disgust when Alice said it hadn't been necessary. "I'm not saying you should be afraid of them, Alice; we know you don't get in trouble. But among other things, you're still our daughter and that's still our house." Even though she protested, they insisted on cutting their weekend short. Alice was sorry their visit was ruined, but she was just as glad they were coming home. She didn't want to sleep in an empty house that night.

Explaining things wasn't easy. When they arrived, her father was still angry that the police had questioned a minor without her parents' permission. Alice tried to tell him about Higgins's offer to wait for her parents, but he brushed it aside.

"Sure, he said that, but he knew good and well you wouldn't." Her dad ran a hand through his thinning hair. "Tell a kid she's too young, to wait for Mommy and Daddy, and she'll talk your ears off. They were probably talking to half the kids at school." His face flushed as he continued, "And they probably tried that same trick on every kid whose parents weren't home. No reason to think you were the only one, but I'm sorry you let them pull your strings that way, honey."

Alice didn't mention the more ominous offer of waiting for a lawyer. She knew Higgins hadn't been talking to every kid in school, but she had no idea how to tell her parents that she was a suspect. You couldn't say, "Hey, folks, guess what, the cops think I'm a burglar and maybe mixed up in a murder."

Her mother had a different question. She'd been thinking, ignoring the question of police propriety while she puzzled it out. "Alice, you said the Raineys? Isn't she the woman who had to leave the Summer Festival concert? The one with the screaming child? I remember you saying she took him every place, and that she didn't even try to get a sitter for the Festival. You don't know her that well; I think you only sat there a few times. Why would the police want to talk to you about it? I doubt if they went around to all the kids, asking questions."

"I wouldn't be surprised if they did," her father said. "Anslow isn't used to murders; they're going to do anything they can to solve it."

"Mom?" Alice braced herself. "There's more to it than that. *I* was supposed to be sitting for Mrs. Rainey. I forgot to write it on the calender." There was a big calendar on the fridge, one that could be written on with a marker and then erased. She always wrote her jobs on it, but this once she'd forgotten. She couldn't have picked a worse time. "When Ryan asked me out, I canceled."

Her mother turned pale as her father went red, bellowing, "What?"

"When did you cancel? You didn't mention turning down a job for a date. Why didn't you tell me?"

"I'm sorry, Mom! I just forgot, and when Ryan asked me out, there seemed no sense in mentioning it. Anyway, that was why I was late getting home from school yesterday. I stopped and told Mrs. Rainey I couldn't sit."

Her mother's face grew paler. If Alice hadn't canceled till Friday afternoon, it was obvious why the police had been there. Her father hid his disturbed feelings behind an even gruffer voice.

"Well, I see why they wanted to talk to you, then. Not that you could really tell them anything, but I guess it would be routine. Do the police think maybe someone was after that girl?"

"Nancy, Dad. Nancy Ettinger. And no, they don't think it was aimed at her. Just those burglars again."

Her mother was unpinning her hair, a sure sign she had a tension headache. As she shook her head slightly, letting the hair fall loose, she said, "That's strange. I hadn't thought of it before, but we actually know several of the people who've been robbed. Right off hand, I can think of four people you've sat for in the last few months who were on that list in the *Answer* last week. Maybe you'd better cut back on baby-sitting for a while, dear, until they catch whoever it is. We were lucky this time; you weren't there. Poor Mrs. Ettinger."

Alice didn't mention that the newer list of

victims had more than four of her clients on it. She still hadn't figured out a way to tell her parents about the suspicions of the police. She was making excuses, she knew, but they were valid ones. Her folks were tired, and they had cut short a trip they'd been looking forward to. Tomorrow would be soon enough.

Her mom came over and hugged her. "Wonderland's a rough neighborhood these days, I guess. Well, we're home now, and at least you're safe. We'll talk more in the morning. I think we'd better get some supper now, and then turn in early."

Later, while she got ready for bed, Alice thought about the *Alice in Wonderland* jokes she'd grown up hearing. She'd go down a rabbit hole in a minute, if she could find one. The White Rabbit and Mad Hatter were less scary than police questioning and burglars and dead baby-sitters. Wonderland had its advantages.

Maybe as a result of thinking about it, Alice spent the night in Wonderland. But it wasn't less scary. The White Rabbit had Detective Higgins's face. He asked her why she'd stolen his white gloves, Mrs. Munson's knicknacks, and the Queen of Heart's cherry tarts. The Mad Hatter and the March Hare handed her a tea-cup with the Dormouse in it. She thought he was asleep, but his head was crushed in. Wonderland was terrifying and strange. The Queen chased her, screams of "Off with her head!" echoing through the night. At last she was caught by the Higgins-Rabbit, who held her while the Queen brandished a crowbar. Alice struggled to get loose as the Queen came toward her.

Alice woke up sweating, the blankets tangled around her feet. The clock beside her bed showed 4:18. She straightened the covers and lay back down. It was just a silly dream.

The real nightmare reclaimed her in the morning. She hadn't decided how to tell her parents about being a suspect, but it no longer mattered. They already knew.

Mr. Fleming put down the paper as Alice entered the kitchen. On Sundays they took the Pueblo newspaper as well as the *Answer*, but he was reading the local news. Yesterday's paper lay beside him on the table as well, opened to the list of crimes on page thirteen.

"Alice. Would you like to explain why you didn't tell us about this last night?" He indicated the list. "The police actually consider you a suspect, don't they? Why didn't you tell us?" His voice was quiet, the quiet that came before an explosion.

"I didn't want to upset you." As soon as she said it, she knew it sounded stupid.

"*Upset* us? Why didn't you think of that before you got mixed up in all of this!"

"Dad, I'm not!" Alice considered running back upstairs and hiding under the covers. "I have no idea who's behind any of this. That's what I told the detective yesterday. I didn't know how to tell you what they thought, but it isn't true!"

Her mother silently handed her a cup of coffee. No greeting, no hug, but at least there was coffee. Alice held the cup between her hands, grateful for the warmth. Her hands felt icy.

Her father shook his head slightly. "Would you mind telling us just what they do think? All we know are the hints this so-called news article has in it." He picked the paper up and read: " 'Unofficial police sources report that a link has been found between the robberies. A single unidentified juvenile, reportedly female, has been employed for child care at various times by all of the victimized households. The police have been questioning the juvenile involved.' " He tossed the paper down.

"Baby-sitting. Every one of the names on that list is one we recognize. You were sup-

83

posed to be at the Raineys' that night. Care to tell us anything else the police said?"

Alice sat down, feeling frustrated and near tears. "Dad, I swear it's all a mistake. Since I canceled so late, Detective Higgins thought that *I* thought Mrs. Rainey wouldn't be able to get another sitter. If I was setting up a break-in, that would give me a nice empty house. They think whoever broke in was surprised to find Nancy there, and they killed Nancy by accident. The cops may be right about that; I don't know. That's the point, Dad: *I don't know.* I don't know who's been breaking into those houses, but it wasn't me! I've baby-sat for so many people in town, it all just has to be a coincidence. Pick any family with kids, odds are I've baby-sat for them."

"But why would the burglars just pick on families with small children?" Her mother sat down beside her. "Sweetheart, I don't think you're a murderer, of course not. But if it's all just a coincidence, wouldn't they have robbed some houses without kids? Or where the kids are older—classmates of yours? Dear, I think someone must be using you. Maybe you've told a friend about hiding places for jewelry . . ." She stopped as Alice shook her head.

"Uh *uh*. Mom, I know better than that! I

never told anybody about that sort of stuff and why would I anyway? Baby-sitting isn't exactly what my friends and I spend our time talking about."

"Maybe not. But if one of them asked you specifically?"

Her father added, "Alice, you aren't doing anybody any favors by covering up for them. If someone was pumping you for information, you'd better tell the cops now."

"No one was. I swear it!"

Her mother's voice held an undercurrent of doubt. "Well, you've never lied to us—that I know of. I guess we'll have to believe you." *For now.*

EIGHT

After she escaped her parents' inquisition at breakfast, Alice retreated to her bedroom. She spent the day leafing through college catalogs and attempting to write a paper for her history class. But every time she picked up her pen her mind began to drift. She couldn't believe this was happening to her; she'd never done anything even remotely illegal in her life, and now the police thought she might be a killer. By the time Ryan called, Alice had written only half a page.

"Alice? Look, about the other night, I'm sorry. . . ."

"Don't worry about it. I'm sorry, too. Let's forget about it, okay?" Alice had wanted to call him on Saturday, but their fight left her reluctant to do so. Now his voice, hesitant and apologetic, sounded wonderful. "Did you hear about Nancy?"

"Yeah. Was she a friend of yours?"

"No, I barely knew her. But that was why I wanted to go home all of a sudden—I heard about the robbery. And you know, I should have been there."

"You what!" It was a half question, half exclamation.

"I canceled that sitting job for our date. When I heard they'd been robbed, I was upset. And later on, when I found out about Nancy . . ."

"God. You could have been there instead. My God, Alice, it could have been you! Look, I'm coming over."

"No, wait." Abruptly, Alice decided she'd much rather get out of the house than stay in any longer. "Pick me up instead. Let's go out for a drive or something."

A half hour later, Ryan honked outside. Alice ran out as he was climbing out of the car. Meeting her in the middle of the driveway, Ryan held her tightly for several moments. His arms felt protective and she enjoyed the sensation. She wanted a little protection, after the last forty-eight hours, and didn't care about the show they were providing for the neighbors. Finally, they got in the car and took off.

Ryan headed out to the lake. Even in the dead of winter, there was occasionally a fisherman or someone just enjoying the sight of open water and trees that the lake provided. Now, in the pleasant warmth of a mid-October afternoon, several cars were parked. Eddie's Corvette was among them, and Alice looked for him. Ryan parked, and he and Alice got out to walk toward the lake. Eddie and Rita were at their favorite picnic table, the one closest to the boathouse. It was almost at the water's edge, and the slope down from the main picnic area hid it from the parked cars. It was sheltered by a large cottonwood and looked out across the broadest expanse of the lake. Tame ducks, mainly mallards that lived on the lake during the year, were quacking indignantly around them, looking for food.

"Wasn't expecting to see you two." Rita smiled at Alice.

"Alice wanted to get out of the house for a while. I knew you two were here." Ryan reached into the small cooler beneath the table and pulled out a soda. He handed it to Alice and got another for himself. "She wanted some distraction, and I can't blame her. Guess what?

She was supposed to have been at the Raineys' Friday night."

Eddie gave Alice a twisted grin. "Could have been you, huh? Bummer. Or not a bummer, since it wasn't you. Would have been a bummer for me if you'd been there, though. I can see me trying to cheer up these two. It'd be bad enough having Rita upset, but Ryan too?" Eddie laughed mirthlessly, although Alice couldn't see anything funny. Neither could Rita, apparently.

"Eddie, what's wrong with you? It would have been horrible if it had been Alice! The whole thing is horrible enough as it is." She looked out over the lake and repeated, "Horrible."

"Yeah, it was horrible. It happened. At least it wasn't Alice, so relax, will ya? That was the idea when we came out here." Eddie sat on the table behind Rita and started rubbing her shoulders. "Take it easy."

Alice wondered when Eddie or Rita would ask her about her other clients. Everyone else had. She decided not to mention her current role as the leading suspect. The news would come out soon enough. Taking Ryan's hand, she walked down nearer the water. The lake was still beautiful, but the shore was dry and brown with the approach of winter. *Bleak*, she thought. *Good match for the way I'm feeling.* She wondered how many of her friends would stay friends when the suspicions of the police hit the news.

A shout made them turn around. Liz was coming down the slope from the parking lot. She'd been more and more of a pain lately, but Alice couldn't see any polite way of avoiding her. They headed back to join the others.

"My mother decided it was a perfect day for pictures. I'm along as pack mule and model." Liz was wearing designer jeans, a rodeo-style Western shirt, and fancy cowboy boots. Her mother was a photographer and frequently used Liz as a subject. Although Liz often made scornful remarks about her mother's efforts, modeling clearly pleased her. She was striking, if not pretty. "She's setting up now."

"Hi, Liz. Grab a soda." Rita didn't sound very welcoming, and Alice didn't blame her. First she and Ryan, then Liz—if Rita had wanted any privacy with Eddie, she hadn't had much luck.

"Thanks." Liz got a diet cola, then looked at Alice with cold eyes. "I wasn't expecting to find the whole world here. No junk sales today?"

"No." Alice didn't say anything else. After a

moment, Liz sniffed, a fastidious sound of distaste.

"Rita, I need to talk to you." She pulled a reluctant Rita off to one side and started talking rapidly as soon as they were out of earshot. Alice shivered slightly and wished she had a sweatshirt on. The breeze off the water was turning chilly. Or was it Liz's arrival?

"That little snot is getting to be a real pain, you know?" Eddie was looking toward Liz with pure venom. Alice was surprised; she had no idea Eddie disliked Liz that much.

"Liz is okay, she's just a little strange sometimes." Ryan's defense was perfunctory. "Main thing is, she's Rita's friend. She can hang around as long as Rita wants her."

"I notice you don't date her to keep Rita happy. You know that's what she wants." Eddie made a mocking half-bow towards Alice. "Sorry, but you've probably figured it out already."

Alice didn't answer, and Ryan frowned. After a few minutes, Rita and Liz returned. Rita's cheeks were slightly flushed, and her eyes were snapping. Whatever Liz had said, it hadn't pleased her at all.

"Oh, Alice, do you think you'll get any more baby-sitting jobs now?" Liz asked in a sugary voice. "People can be so superstitious about bad luck, don't you think?" Alice's stomach hit freefall as she realized what this meant. Liz's next words confirmed it.

"I hadn't realized you were such a jinx. Tell me, did you really baby-sit for all those people? That's scary. It will spoil some of your plans if you have to give it up, right?"

"Liz, I thought you were modeling for Mama. Don't you think she's ready for you now?" Eddie's voice sounded lazy, with none of the hostility he'd expressed a few moments before. But Alice translated the words silently. *Go tell your mother she wants you.* The classic put-down line to chase away pesky kids.

Liz's tight-lipped smile indicated she'd heard it that way as well. But she shook her head. "Oh, she's playing with filters and stuff. She knows where I am, but I doubt if she'll be ready for me for another half hour. There's time for some fun first. That's old man Kosmayer's boat. I know how to start it. Want to go for a boat ride?" She smirked and looked straight at Eddie.

Behind her, Alice heard Rita's sharp inhalation. Eddie came to the lake often, but he was terrified of water. He couldn't swim, wouldn't even try to learn. He never turned a hair racing

Ryan and the Colorado Highway Patrol, but he couldn't step into a rowboat tied at the dock. Taunting him with a boat ride was like slapping his face.

Eddie's lips were white. His fist came up as he took a half step toward Liz. Rita grabbed his arm and clung to it, holding him back. "Liz, get out of here," she said. "Now."

Liz looked at Eddie. She started to say something, but the look on his face stopped her. "Well, I suppose I have to go model for my mom anyway. Let us know what the police say, Alice." She turned and walked rapidly away, following the curve of the lake out of sight. Rita released Eddie's arm, as Alice released her breath. She hadn't realized she was holding it.

She asked Ryan to take her home. As a distraction, the afternoon hadn't been much of a success.

NINE

During the next week, Alice felt more and more as though she'd wandered into a nightmare Wonderland. It started on Monday. The first draft of her term paper on the Constitutional Convention of 1787 was due for American history. After coming home from the lake on Sunday she totally forgot about the paper; she had too many other things on her mind. A classmate reminded her that morning. Then Alice got into trouble during first-period Spanish for working on the history paper. Alice gave up on trying to complete a weekend of work in her other classes. Maybe at lunch. But that would mean giving up her time with Ryan.

Long before lunchtime, Alice realized something else was wrong. Some of her classmates were avoiding her. There had always been a few who had resented her grades and hard work and who thought she was a brown-nose. She had never been as popular as some of the party kids, like Liz and Rita. But she'd known most of her fellow students her whole life. She had classes with them, joked with them, compared notes with them. Today, she was invisible.

At first Alice had no idea what was going on. The entire school was upset anyway. There was much less noise in the halls than usual, but individual voices were louder. She hadn't been the only one in Spanish class whose attention span had shrunk. Even the Señora had lost her place in *El Nublado Rojo*, the novel they were reading. The absentee rate was as high as it had been during the flu epidemic the year before, and six teachers were out. Students of Anslow Union High had died before, in car wrecks, in hunting and boating accidents, and occasionally of disease. There had never been a murder.

Alice assumed that everyone was just being quiet because they were upset about Nancy. She asked Mike Cordova, captain of the football team and a casual friend, if he'd seen Ryan. He quickly shook his head and walked rapidly away from her. In physics her lab partner handed her his lab notes but left her to set up the experiment by herself. It wasn't until the fourth class of the day that she heard someone whisper, behind her, "baby-sitter."

Baby-sitter. Lots of girls baby-sat occasionally. But Alice did more than anyone else in town. She'd heard them talking about Nancy earlier, and the word "murder." She wished desperately that no one had made the connection to her baby-sitting list. She didn't have much hope.

Lunch killed what little hope she did have, along with her appetite. She gave up her plans to work on the term paper. There really wasn't enough time, and she would rather be with Ryan. But the weather had turned into a chilly gray drizzle, and they had to eat in the cafeteria. Alice sat between Rita and Ryan, with Eddie on the other side of Rita. No one within earshot of them was talking. Beyond, the hum of voices was almost a roar.

After half a dozen bites, Alice wished she'd gone to the library instead. Rita was moody, in a way Alice had never seen before. She would sit, saying nothing for several minutes at a time, then say something so funny, and so cruel, that Alice couldn't help feeling guilty even while laughing. And Eddie's comments matched. Ryan squeezed her hand under the table but didn't speak at all. The scene at the lake the previous day was poisoning the ease she normally felt with the twins and Eddie.

Since they shared a class second period, Alice knew Liz was in school, but she wasn't in the cafeteria. Her absence was the only thing that made the meal bearable. Bearability vanished, however, when Liz came in, talking to Steve. Alice lifted her eyebrows. Usually Liz had nothing but scorn for Steve; she considered him even more of a grub than Alice. Whatever Liz was telling him was important, at least to her; the expression on her face spoke across the noise of the cafeteria. Steve shrugged, obviously not as interested in hearing as Liz was in telling. He said something to her, and her face tightened. Whirling away from him, she crossed the cafeteria to Alice's table. Predictably, she wasn't bothering to eat.

She sat down across from Alice. At first none of them spoke. No one wanted to say out loud what everyone was remembering. Finally, Liz slumped slightly.

"Yeah, well, you all know I have a mouth." It wasn't much of a conversational opener, and less of an apology, but it was enough. They all started talking, carefully avoiding any mention of Nancy. Alice hated it. American history had never looked so appealing. The school tacos tasted like the cardboard the kids always said they were. Lunch felt longer than the normal forty minutes.

The afternoon went on, slightly off-key the entire time. History was almost a relief. There was a substitute. The regular teacher hadn't left adequate notes, as she freely admitted, so she wasn't sure what the class should be doing. She didn't collect the papers; instead, she gave them a free study hall. Most kids talked quietly in small groups. Alice got busy on her draft and had it almost completed by the end of the period.

No one spoke to Alice as she walked to her locker. She got most of her books out, although it would make her book bag almost impossibly heavy. To top the day off, she didn't even have a ride home. Ryan and Eddie were tied up with something for the Athletics Club. She walked home alone through the cold misty rain.

Neither the weather nor her mood had improved by morning. She skimmed through the paper, unable to focus on any of the articles. Even the funnies seemed totally unfunny, and none rated the smallest smile. The *Anslow Answer* was full of portentous hints, indications that they were in the complete confidence of the police, who had the robberies all but solved. Alice shook her head. The police thought she was part of the solution. If the police "solved" the case the way they were headed right now, she'd be arrested for murder.

Alice left her mother reading an editorial about the need for a fast arrest. Earlier she'd heard her mom calling in to work to take a sick day. Her mom wasn't really ill, not with a virus or anything a doctor could help. She was worried sick, and Alice felt guilty for causing the anxiety. But she hadn't *done* anything. Why didn't anyone believe her?

The mood at school had turned nastier. The first person she saw when she walked in was Liz, talking to Mike Cordova. He looked at her wide-eyed. She decided the horns Liz was accusing her of having must be visible. That was how people were acting, in any case. Liz's jealousy wasn't anything new, but these tactics were. She wasn't going to stop seeing Ryan just to shut Liz up. It was pretty rotten of her to use Nancy's death like this.

It was still raining at lunch time so they had to eat inside again. Rita and Eddie were off someplace, so she had Ryan to herself. He acted as though everything were normal. Alice actually enjoyed her lunch, until Liz sat down beside them.

"Did you see the paper this morning, Alice? They had the dollar amount on all the loot stolen in all those robberies. Honestly, it's hard to think of all that junk being worth anything, but it really added up. I bet that's more than you make baby-sitting in a year."

Alice could feel her face going red, but this time it wasn't embarrassment. An angry flush and a blush looked alike, but they didn't feel the same. "I'm surprised you bother reading the paper beyond the fashion page. But you spend so much money, you ought to have some idea of how much things cost. Unless you never even look."

Liz grinned, with a nasty edge. "Why should I? I can't buy everything, of course, but I know where to go and where not to. Maybe that's your trouble, Alice. You don't know where you should just *stay out*."

Ryan took a deep breath. Alice could feel the tension in his arm muscles. When he spoke, however, his voice sounded calm. "I haven't seen Alice ignoring any keep out signs. And the only thing she wants to get into is college."

"Yeah, we've all heard so much about how hard Alice works and how much she wants to go and how dedicated she is and on and on and on. Makes me want to puke, to tell the truth. Well, I think maybe she got a little too determined. She wanted it so badly she did anything she could to get the money." She glared at Alice, then stood up. Not giving either of them a chance to answer, she whirled on her heel and was gone.

Alice bent her head forward, staring at the table and letting her hair fall over her face. There was a shred of truth in Liz's words. Some people did make too much of her school work and her ambition. But she had just done the work; she hadn't asked for the applause. She shouldn't have to feel guilty for doing better than others when she'd earned it.

"Hey. Get the head up, kiddo." Ryan's hand gently brushed the tears that had begun to fall off her cheek. "You don't want people to think there's any truth to that crap, do you? I know you haven't done anything. So just ignore her."

Alice tossed her hair back from her face. Liz could try to turn everyone against her, but it wouldn't work. Ryan believed her; that was a good start. If everyone in the lunchroom wanted to stare at her runny eyeliner, let them. She'd done nothing to be ashamed of. She had to stop in the restroom and fix her make-up before class started, though. A firm chin and melted mascara didn't go together.

Her resolve lasted through the final class of the day. Then it crumbled along with her remaining dreams. The week before, she had been called into the counselor's office for the news about the scholarship. Now Mrs. Komax called her in again. Once more, the subject was the scholarship. But this time, it wasn't good news.

"Postponed? Mrs. Komax, how can they postpone making the official recommendation? Without it, I won't get the scholarship at all!"

"Alice, it's just been tabled temporarily." The counselor avoided Alice's eyes, aware of how thin the excuse was. "The council decided there were some unanswered questions about this . . . this tragedy with Nancy. I'm sure, in a few weeks when the police find out who was responsible, they'll go ahead and approve the official recommendation."

"But the deadline . . ."

"I'm so sorry, Alice." Mrs. Komax really did look sorry about it. "But the vote was to table any decision. There's still time." They both knew how little time there really was.

"Why?" Alice knew the reason, but she wondered if Mrs. Komax did. That would be an indication of how widely the story had spread.

Mrs. Komax was a good counselor, able to face tough questions. This was probably the first time she'd been faced with one such as this. She squeezed the bridge of her nose for a moment, as though she had a headache, then leveled with Alice. "It isn't anything official, Alice. And the request was made that it be kept unofficial for the time being. But someone from the police told the council president that you're under suspicion for the burglaries. Which means you may be involved in Nancy's death. Apparently, all of the victims . . ." She broke off. "You know all this. The council felt they couldn't give you the recommendation right now."

"Because I'm supposed to be a murderer and a thief." Alice was bitter. Mrs. Komax sighed.

"I don't believe that, Alice. But there certainly are questions. You know that."

"Yeah. Questions I can't answer." For the second time that day, she started crying. This time, she didn't hide it.

"Alice, if there's anything you do need to say, anything you're afraid to tell the police on your own, anyone you're afraid of . . ." Mrs. Komax's kindness was, in a way, more painful than Liz's earlier hatefulness. Even the people who wanted to believe in Alice were convinced she was holding something back. She wished she were; then at least she'd know the answers to everyone's questions.

Alice left the school, heading for her Tuesday sitting job at the Munsons'. She didn't look for Ryan. This blow hurt too much; she couldn't even face sympathy yet. She walked slowly, trying to understand how her life could have fallen apart in a single week.

Her miserable day wasn't done yet. When she arrived at the Munsons', Tyler was glad to see her, and started to tell her all about their house being on TV. The excitement still predominated for him, Alice was glad to see. But Mrs. Munson was unusually cold. She sent Tyler into the family room, while she talked to Alice.

"Alice, I'm afraid we won't be needing you for a while." Mrs. Munson wasn't as embarrassed as Mrs. Komax had been. "I've heard some rumors—well, I'm sorry, but I think it might be better all around if we canceled for the next few weeks."

"You think I had something to do with it." It wasn't really a question, more like a plea for reassurance. "Mrs. Munson, I didn't. I wish you'd believe me."

"I'd like to. But until the police settle this, I think this will be better for Tyler."

Alice walked home exhausted and beyond tears. She was alive, but her future was as dead as Nancy. Years of working and studying were wasted because of someone else. And she had no idea who. That was almost the worst of it. Whoever had wrecked her life was still invisible, to her and to the police. There was one major difference. She knew there had to be someone else. The police didn't.

Her mother was surprised to see her at home. Alice told her the news, reciting the facts as dryly as newspaper statistics. Her mother bit her lip, fighting her own tears. She looked a question at Alice when she finished speaking.

"No, Mom," she said tiredly. "I still don't know anything about it. If it's more than a coincidence, someone forgot to tell me." She turned and went to her room.

That night she was back in the room with no door—the one she'd dreamed about before Nancy's murder. She walked into the room, closed the door, and the door melted, blending into the wall without a trace. She started looking for a way out. One thing had changed from her previous dream. This time, little by little, the walls were slowly moving inward. When they reached the center, Alice would be crushed.

TEN

The bad dreams continued, echoing the nightmare that had engulfed her waking life. The next two days at school brought no relief. Alice went through the motions in her classes, no longer sure it was worth anything.

Ryan, at least, acted as though nothing had changed. He took her to Geponi's for pizza Wednesday evening, ignoring the stares from the crowd in the restaurant. The pepperoni tasted stale; nothing had really tasted good for a week, but she was sharing it in public with someone who believed her. There weren't many left who did.

Thursday morning she found another supporter. Jan Robbins came up to her before Spanish. Jan was part of her old crowd—the kids she had hung out with back when she'd been going out with Steve. Alice hadn't seen much of her since she'd been dating Ryan.

"Hi, Alice. Hey, have the cops really been questioning you?"

"Yeah, they have." Alice stiffened herself for a putdown.

"That's ridiculous. I mean, you're too smart to be that stupid."

"Thanks." Alice's smile was half relief, half rueful grimace. "I haven't had much luck convincing people of that. Even my parents think I must have said something to someone."

Jan shrugged. "Yeah, it's a wild coincidence. But even if it's more than a coincidence, it still doesn't mean you know who killed Nancy."

"Figure out a way for me to convince the police. And my folks. And the city council, for that matter; my scholarship is on hold."

"That's lousy." The warning bell rang, and Jan turned to go. "Wish I could help, but I don't even know any of the people who got robbed. Don't let it get to you, Alice." She vanished into the room across the hall, and Alice barely made it to her seat in time.

It was nice of Jan to go out of her way like that, considering what she thought of Rita and Ryan and the rest of Alice's new friends. She'd made her opinion of them clear some time ago. At least some people didn't think Alice was a killer. Although even Jan thought there was more than coincidence involved. Maybe there was.

A few other kids asked Alice questions. She was happy to talk about it, since it was the only way she could fight rumors. By Thursday afternoon, she'd heard them all indirectly. She was everything from a bloody-handed murderer right out of the latest slasher movie to a Moriarity mastermind who had organized a burglary ring that reached clear to Denver. *Maybe I need to get some buttons made up,* she thought. She doodled possible mottos on the edge of her math notebook. *Don't Ask Me; Ask the Cops,* for example. Or *I Don't Know Anything Either.* It wouldn't stop the rumors, though; nothing would.

Surprisingly enough, Liz was halfway civil. Since the damage was already done, she could now act polite. Alice suspected Rita had told her to lay off. If that was the case, it was too little too late. Once rumors started, they kept going on their own. She should do a physics project on rumors as a form of perpetual motion.

That night she had a job that amazingly

hadn't been canceled. Ryan gave her a ride home and a quick kiss before he roared off. By the time her mom got home from work, Alice had macaroni and cheese ready for supper. Her mom made a salad and garlic bread while Alice got her books together for the walk over to the Eisens' house. Her dad came in just as the bread came out of the oven. To Alice's dismay, he wasn't alone; Steve was with him. All week long he'd been hanging around her at school, but not saying anything. It was getting on her nerves.

"Hi, Steve. Want some supper?" Her mom was putting on an extra plate even as she spoke.

"I ate already, but I could eat some of that garlic bread." He sat down in the spare chair, while her dad went to wash up. "Your dad pulled in just ahead of me." He went on, talking of nothing in particular while Alice wondered why he'd come.

Over the meal, she found out. "Mr. Fleming, what I came over for, there's going to be a street fair in Pueblo next year. I think they're trying for some of the history buffs; they're talking about Zebulon Pike and the fur traders." He grinned. "Which lets them talk about Pike's Peak or Bust, the gold rush days, and the frontier. Even if it isn't much of a connection, it's good enough for a fair theme."

"And maybe the silver days? Hmm, there'd be a good tie-in for some gold nugget stuff." Her father stared into space for a moment, then nodded. "Yeah, that sounds as though it might be worth looking in to. How much are permits or booths going to be? And how'd you find out about it?"

Steve brushed that aside. "I was in town; someone I know mentioned it and I got some information for you. They're still setting it up; you might be able to get in on the planning instead of being just another street seller." He dug a crumpled letter and flyer out of his hip pocket and handed them across the table.

The rest of the meal was spent weighing possibilities, trying to decide what would sell best to the tourists the fair was aimed at. Her dad couldn't make a living at his metal work and jewelry, but it was his passion. It was nice of Steve to have told him about the fair, but Alice was suspicious. She got ready to leave for her sitting job, waiting for Steve to say something that would show the real reason he was here.

"You going someplace, Alice? It's raining again." She looked out the window to confirm his weather report. Even the weather was unreal. This much rain in October? "I'll give you a lift, no sense getting soaked."

"Thanks. I'm just going to the Eisens' house." She hadn't been alone with Steve since the day of the questioning. She didn't want to accept a ride from him, but there was no way of telling her parents that. As her dad would say, it wasn't practical. A few minutes later, they left together. The light rain was mixed with fog, growing thicker by the moment.

"You hear the latest on the burglaries?" Steve tried to look past the additional fog on the inside of the windshield, rubbing at it with one hand. The defroster wasn't cutting through the thick condensation and it was hard to see through the windshield. "Some of the stuff's started showing up in Pueblo. The cops got it today. They think they can trace it back. No way, though."

Alice dug a tissue out of her knapsack and reached in front of Steve to wipe the glass. She didn't want to end up in a ditch, no matter how lousy the week had been. "Why? What'd they find? And how do you know anything about it?"

"Some of the stuff from the Munson job, those pearls you kept talking about. They showed up at Second Chance Sam's."

"Mrs. Munson will get her pearls back!" For

a moment that was the only part that sank in. "Wait a sec—Sam's? What good does that do?" The fog formed again as soon as Alice stopped wiping.

"Exactly." Second Chance Sam's was an everything store. He sold jewelry, he did a little pawnbroking, he handled a lot of secondhand. Alice had sold things there for her father, and she occasionally purchased junk jewelry. Steve checked it for electronics regularly. Even though Alice and her dad neither liked or trusted Sam, it was hard to avoid doing some business with him.

"He really had that necklace on display and he didn't have the records on it? I thought even Sam knew better than that. That's too big an item to not have IDs on."

The defroster was finally doing a little good. Steve peered out through the small fan-shaped area of clear glass. "Sure, *if* it had been in the store on display. The Pueblo police were checking something else, and it showed up. On Mrs. Sam's neck. Or an almost-Mrs. Sam, anyway. He said he bought it off a guy with a Chicago address. And the guy had such an honest face. . . ."

"Yeah, right." Sam had used stories like that for years. No one ever believed them, but there was usually no way of proving them lies, either. There were strict laws for pawnshops; supposedly nothing could be purchased without proof of ID of the seller. Honest shops kept careful records. Sam and the ones like him figured the fines they paid were overhead.

"Anyway, the Pueblo cops spotted it from the list and called Higgins. They might close Sam down this time." Steve pulled up in front of the Eisens' sprawling house and sat there. "Anyway, I just wondered if you knew about it."

"I'm not in the confidence of the police the way you seem to be," she said. She wanted to know why Steve had told her all this. "I'm happy Mrs. Munson will get the necklace back."

"Yeah. That one seemed to upset you." He stared through the windshield, which was misting over again now that the defroster was off. "I wondered if it would bother you, that's all. Since you do business with Sam all the time."

"Why should it? I didn't have anything to do with those robberies, and I'm tired of people saying I did! You do business with him yourself." She opened the door and got out, then stood for a moment, holding it. "Thanks for the ride, and thanks for giving Dad that stuff about the fair. Where'd you get it, anyway?"

"From Sam. I was in there today." He reached over and pulled the door shut, then roared off down the street, leaving her staring after him.

Two hours later Alice had curled up on the comfortable couch in the Eisens' family room, reading a book. She had finished her homework, and the Eisens weren't due back for another hour and a half. She'd enjoyed the quiet evening; the bedtime story, the calm, normal routines of baby-sitting. She was glad the Eisens hadn't mentioned the burglaries. They must trust her.

Or else they didn't watch the news or read the papers.

Alice had brought along some tapes and had them on softly, since little Shannon was a light sleeper. As one tape finished and clicked off, she folded a corner of a page down, yawned, and got up to change it. In the sudden stillness, she heard a noise.

The doors were locked, and Mrs. Eisen had pointed out the safety chains. They were on. Nancy had thought she was safe in a locked house. Alice froze, listening intently. Something was moving around on the back patio, and she didn't think it was a squirrel or raccoon.

She tiptoed into the kitchen without flipping

the light switch and paused just inside the doorway. Was that shadow moving? She fumbled along the wall for the row of light switches. Her fingers felt past the first two, the main kitchen lights, and the third one, which lit the entrance hall. There. The fourth and fifth switches controlled the floodlights on the back patio. Flipping them, she then ducked back into the family room. If there *was* someone out there, Alice would be just as happy if he got away.

After a few minutes, she returned to the darkened kitchen and peered out into the back yard. There was nothing on the patio, and the rest of the yard was invisible beyond the range of the floodlights. She went to get the long metal flashlight the Eisens kept in the coat closet. Coming back, she flipped the floods off, then shone the powerful light outside. Nothing there. The fog had settled back into a drizzle, making it hard to see. The only thing Alice saw was the soggy remnants of Mrs. Eisen's fall flower garden. Then her throat clamped shut as she saw a figure by the back fence.

She couldn't make it out clearly in the thickening mist. Whoever it was ducked back behind a row of bushes when the light hit. But there was definitely someone there; it wasn't just her nerves on a rainy night. Alice wasn't going to wait for the prowler to come to her. It might not be the same one who killed Nancy, but she was calling the police. Now.

She tightened her grip on the heavy flashlight. It would serve as light and weapon both. Crossing back to the family room, Alice turned on all the lights as she entered, and then picked up the phone. She dialed 911 and in a few quick words told the calm voice on the other end that there was a prowler outside, please send someone, this address, thank you. She hung up seconds before the shatter of breaking glass exploded from the kitchen.

Alice screamed. As if in answer, Shannon began to wail. More tinkles of falling and breaking glass came from the kitchen, as Shannon's voice echoed down the stairwell.

"*Mom-m-m-meeee!*" The terror in the five-year-old's voice galvanized Alice and she sprang for the stairs, still gripping the flashlight as though it were a club. She rushed into the child's room, flipping on the light as she entered. The little girl was sitting up in bed, holding her teddy bear. Alice shut the door, then dragged the heavy rocker in front of it. The child's eyes grew still wider at this barricading of the door. Alice sank down onto the bed and took the girl in her arms, rocking her as though she was a baby.

They sat that way for almost five minutes. Alice was comforted by the solid weight of the child in her arms. Shannon was real, not a shadowy phantom out in the mist. Finally, Alice relaxed a bit. The noise must have scared him off.

Alice didn't tell Shannon the scream and breaking glass were real. She assured the child several times that bad dreams couldn't hurt her. Shannon didn't ask about the rocker, and Alice figured it was safer to ignore it as well. It would be difficult explaining why she'd blocked the door against imaginary fears.

Leaving the hall light on, Alice headed back down the stairs, once more holding the flashlight in her hand in case her own bad dream managed to break in. She was almost to the foot of the stairs when she heard the faint wail of a siren. The police arrived moments later, lights flashing. If the prowler hadn't been scared off by her scream and Shannon's shrieks, he surely was by this conspicuous arrival. Alice ran back upstairs, trying to calm a re-frightened Shannon. When the police pounded on the door, she scooped the girl up in her arms and carried her downstairs with her.

The next quarter of an hour was a study in

madness to make the Mad Hatter's Tea Party look mild. Shannon had settled into a state of near-hysterics, which Alice tried to quell while simultaneously attempting to answer questions from the police. Some semblance of order was imposed, with the arrival of Mr. and Mrs. Eisen. They took Shannon up to bed and Mrs. Eisen stayed with her, while Mr. Eisen returned to monitor the police questions. Shannon's sobs finally faded away, as the police asked Alice to describe the evening yet again.

". . . and when I was sure I really saw him I went in and called 911."

"You say 'him.' I thought you couldn't see the figure that clearly?" The uniformed man was carefully writing down each word Alice uttered. He had looked sharply at her when she had given her name. Of course, she thought bitterly, it's known around the police headquarters by now.

"I couldn't. I just assumed it was male, but honestly, it could have been anyone."

"And the window was broken . . . when?"

"Right after I hung up." She was glad at least it wasn't Higgins, but she had no doubt he would be getting a full report the first thing in the morning.

As the questioning went on, Alice began to

feel sick to her stomach. They didn't believe her. The glass she had heard shattering was from the window next to the back door. It lay in shards all over the counter and floor. But there was nothing to show what had been used to break it, no rock on the ground or inside the kitchen. Nothing. It would have been easy for Alice to open the back door, break the window so the glass fell into the house, and then relock and chain the door. She'd read enough Agatha Christies and watched enough *Columbo* reruns to know the pattern. It always happened in the second quarter hour of the show; the villain would fake a crime so that he or she would appear to be the target. It had never occurred to Alice that the same sort of thing really could happen to an innocent victim.

Mr. Eisen hadn't said much during the entire time they were asking questions, but his face had grown increasingly grimmer. Finally, there were sounds of another car outside, and the officer who'd been questioning Alice left the room. Alice hung her head, but she could feel Mr. Eisen watching her.

"Alice, I don't know what to say. We heard the rumors, but we didn't believe them." Alice raised her head at this, appalled. They *had* known, and they had trusted her anyway. And now—oh, please, God, no. Mr. Eisen coughed, then continued. "I'm afraid we can't ask you to work for us anymore. I know you say there was a prowler, but, frankly . . . Alice, I don't know what we can believe anymore."

Once more, her head was down, her hair now concealing her face completely and with it, the tears. "I'll pay for the window."

"That won't be necessary. Here . . ." He pulled out his wallet and paid her enough to cover the evening at her full rate, even the time spent with the police. She tried to turn it down, but he insisted, as though he refused to be indebted to her in any way.

The officer who'd been asking Alice questions came back in, followed by a newcomer. It was Detective Higgins. Obviously they'd gotten him out of bed for this one, and they'd already brought him up to date. The routine started again, covering the same tired ground, but this time Higgins asked the questions.

The session was mercifully brief. At last Higgins said Alice was free to go. She turned awkwardly to Mr. Eisen. She hated to ask him for a ride, but it was much too late for her to walk. Before he could say anything, Higgins volunteered. Alice didn't want a ride from the Grand

Inquisitor, but a look at Mr. Eisen's tight face changed her mind.

They rode in silence most of the way. She was profoundly grateful for that much. As they approached her home, Higgins broke the tense stillness.

"You know, I think you're a good kid who got yourself in over your head. You have a rep for hard work. You just got a little too hungry for some cash, and you got mixed in with the wrong people. Let me tell you something, Alice. You didn't see Nancy with her head bashed in like that, but it wasn't pretty. And the same thing might happen to you if you don't level with us. You may think your friends wouldn't do that to you. Well, tell Nancy that, or Nancy's parents."

He stopped in the Flemings' driveway. "If you tell us who's in this with you, I think we can arrange a deal. You're still a juvenile. The law lets us try you as an adult on a serious enough crime, and this is. But we don't have to. As a juvenile you'd draw a lighter sentence and have a chance to start fresh again someday. What do you say, Alice?"

She shook her head. She had nothing to say. After a few minutes he sighed. She got out and stood there for a moment. Finally, she gave a little shrug and headed inside. It was hopeless.

ELEVEN

By Saturday the weather had reverted to the warmth of a Colorado Indian summer. Winter wasn't far off, but there were traces of summer foliage left, and the skies were again blue. The mountains to the west were dusted with fresh snow from the storms of the past few days. It was a day to be outside, and when her father asked her if she wanted to go with him to the flea market, Alice eagerly agreed. The tension had been worse at home than anyplace else. Her parents' doubt had been the hardest part of the past week.

Just as they were getting ready to leave, the phone rang.

"You been out today?" It was Ryan. "It's a good day for a drive. I thought we might head toward the mountains, maybe clear up to Colorado Springs. You want to?"

She was torn. "Ryan, would you mind if we did something else? Dad asked me to go with him to the flea market, and I already said yes. How about meeting us there? I'll spend a couple hours with Dad, and then we can split. It's halfway to Pueblo. . . ." She left it hanging.

"Yeah, all right. Look, I was thinking we'd catch up with Rita and Eddie later on. Let me set it up with them, all right?"

"Great. You know where my dad usually works, on the west side. I'll see you there." She hung up. Her mom handed her the thermos and sketched a kiss in mid-air as Alice ran out to the pickup. Her dad had already started it. Alice set the thermos carefully at her feet and buckled her seatbelt as he backed out of the driveway. She felt better. Obviously her folks didn't consider her a cold-blooded killer. Things would work out—eventually.

They had to.

For the first few miles, she pushed all thoughts of the past week to the back of her mind as they talked about her mother's birthday present. Dad was making a new set of earrings for her and he hadn't decided whether to use peridots or Apache tears. Alice voted for peridots and rolled down her window. Terror was far away.

A faint whiff of trouble returned, however, as her father changed the subject. He fortified himself by gulping down half a cup of coffee, then asked her, "Honey, have you thought any more about what Detective Higgins said?" Higgins had talked to her parents on Friday, repeating his offer of leniency. Last night they'd begged her to tell him what he wanted to know. It had turned into an argument, ending with shouts and slammed doors. The dawn of a sunny day had put an end of it, or so she'd hoped.

"Dad, I wish there were something I *could* say." She didn't intend to resurrect the fight. Maybe now, with the warm autumn air blowing through the truck, he'd listen. "I don't really enjoy having everybody looking at me like I was a monster. Especially you and Mom. If there was anything *to* tell, believe me, I would."

His mouth tightened, but he seemed as determined as she was to avoid a blowup. "Don't you think we *want* to believe you? It just that there are an awful lot of things that need explaining."

Alice watched a few miles of scenery before replying. "There *are* too many coincidences. I didn't think so at first, but maybe you're right. Maybe Detective Higgins is right." In her mind, she heard the Eisens' kitchen window shatter again. That night she'd accepted the idea she really was involved. But she still had no idea of how.

Her father sighed, then started talking about the plans for the tourist fair in Pueblo that Steve had told them about. Dad had gotten more information and his enthusiasm was growing. Alice let him do most of the talking, while she tried to recapture her earlier feeling of peace. She didn't succeed completely, since the conversation kept Steve on her mind. He'd found out about the fair from Sam. Why had he been talking to Sam in the first place? And had Sam said anything to the police yet about where he'd gotten Mrs. Munson's pearls?

Her enjoyment of the day slipped a notch when they arrived at the Flea Circus. The first person they saw after reaching their space was Steve. Alice suspected he'd been waiting for them. They were easy enough to find, since her dad always had a spot in the same general area. And it would match the way he'd been hovering around her all week. Her dad welcomed Steve expansively, starting at once to talk again about the fair. Her own greeting was perfunctory. Her dad looked at her in mild surprise, but finished what he was saying about probable attendance.

". . . that's just a rough estimate, of course. Pueblo doesn't have the tourists Denver does, or Aspen, but a few more special events like this would improve things."

"It might. Sure couldn't hurt any." Steve turned to speak to her. "Alice, did the police ever find any evidence of a prowler the other night? I mean, besides the busted window."

She was surprised, at first, since there'd been no mention of the episode in the news. No one at school had asked any questions about it, and she had hoped it would remain private. Then she remembered Steve and his scanner. Still, it was uncanny the way he always seemed to know just what was going on.

"I told you before. The police haven't taken me into their confidence. Of course, I shouldn't complain," Alice added dryly. "They haven't taken me into custody yet, either. But you seem to know a lot more about what they're doing than I do." She began to arrange the display of her father's jewelry. Steve moved to help her and she started to tell him she could manage on her own, then stole a look at her dad and decided against it.

In a lower tone, pitched just for Alice's ears,

Steve said, "I'm not exactly in their confidence either. I just hear things sometimes. But I haven't heard anything further on that prowler. I don't think they believe there was one, Alice."

"That's no surprise." Despite her best attempt to speak normally, she found her voice coming from between clenched teeth. "Even the people who think I'm not a thief think I'm a liar. Even my parents. Everybody but Ryan."

"Oh, sure, Ryan believes every word you say. Like that really means a lot. Look, just because someone doesn't buy your whole story doesn't mean they're out to get you. Maybe they just want to help you."

"And maybe I don't want their help! I don't want yours, that's for sure!" She straightened up, glaring at him. Her voice was no longer the careful undertone she'd started with, and she knew her dad was staring at her, but she didn't care. "I just wish you'd leave me alone. All of you!"

His face as angry as hers, Steve replied, "Why do you keep pushing me away?"

"Maybe you're too pushy. Ever think of that? Steve, we aren't going out anymore. What happens to me is none of your business. And stop watching me!"

"Watching you?"

"Yes, watching! Every time I turn around, there you are. I don't know what you think you're doing, but it's getting on my nerves. Just cut it out."

Her father made shushing noises as the people in the next space were looking at them. Alice quickly turned back to setting up the display on the table. Her father got the poles and canvas from the truck and started setting up the small awning they used for shade. He shot several sharp glances her way, clearly wanting an explanation. She ducked her head, realizing as she did so that the ponytail she wore today didn't provide a curtain to hide behind.

While they worked, Steve and her dad talked in low tones. Somehow Alice didn't think it was about the fair this time. They were discussing her "story." No one saw it as simple truth. She didn't want to be put through another cross-examination. With forced casualness, she said, "Hey, Dad, I'm going to wander around for a while. If Ryan gets here, I'll be over by the dealers' stalls, okay?" She hurried off without waiting for a reply.

As soon as she was out of their sight, she slowed her pace. Liz could make comments about junk peddlers if she wanted to. Alice had been an occasional inhabitant of this world for much of her life and she enjoyed it. It wasn't elegant, but it was always fascinating. She browsed through a carton of used books some people had in the trunk of their car, then stopped a few spaces down to check out some bead jewelry. She found a rock hound, with some raw stone for sale, and made a note of the location. Her father would be interested.

Alice reached the center of the market where the two major rows crossed. Almost at the intersection was one of the largest permanent booths at the Flea Circus. Alice didn't like old Stoneman, or trust him, but his booth always had one of the widest varieties of goods for sale. She went into the crowded stall and began looking at the used books, her usual first stop, working her way toward his jewelry. She had already spotted a malachite necklace on display that she thought was her dad's handiwork. Stoneman sometimes bought from them directly. More often things made their way through several hands before turning up here. She couldn't remember who had bought the necklace, but she would bet Stoneman was getting three times what her father had. She put down the tattered paperback she was looking at and moved closer.

At the end of the improvised bookshelf was another counter, crowded with glassware. The jewelry was just beyond. Her eyes roamed over the chipped cups and cheap candlesticks, then stopped. She stared, frozen, at a small piece of nightmare escaped from the past week of bad dreams.

Almost without thinking, she picked it up. It was a simple thing, certainly not something to inspire terror. It was a small crystal cat paperweight. A small white tag was stuck to the bottom, a price marked on it in blue ink. Near the tip of the tail there was a tiny chip. Alice remembered where she'd seen it before. It had been on an end table in Mrs. Rainey's living room the day Nancy had been murdered.

Alice tightened her grip. It was weird that the burglars had stolen such a worthless item, but very little of value had been taken from the Raineys. The police theory, which she'd read dozens of times in news accounts, was that the killing occurred almost immediately after the crooks broke in. The cat could have been grabbed easily while the robbers were fleeing.

Alice looked around for Stoneman, wondering if he could tell her anything about where the cat came from. Or if he would. Alice knew that the cat could have already passed through a dozen hands, even in this short time. It was probably hopeless. But she could try. Any sort of clue to the real killers would help.

"Mr. Stoneman?" Her heart sank. A nearby booth sold beer, and from the smell the old man had drunk several. Mr. Stoneman was known around the Flea Circus as a mean drunk. "I wonder if you could tell me anything about this paperweight?"

He scowled and squinted at her. "I seen you in here before, ain't I? Yeah, your old man's the one does the necklaces. Good work. What?" He refocused on the object she was holding out to him. "It's a cat. Real crystal. Make you a good price on it if you want it."

"I wanted to find out where you got it. Do you know who sold it to you, Mr. Stoneman?"

His blood-shot eyes grew suspicious. "Why, what the hell difference does that make? Naw, I don't know who I got it off of. It's been laying around here for a month or so."

That was that, then. If he didn't want to tell her anything, she was stymied. She knew the cat hadn't been there for weeks. Stoneman either honestly didn't remember, or he remembered and didn't intend to tell. Either way, it was a dead end.

"You want the thing or not? I ain't got time to stand around here tryin' to figure out where in

Hades all this junk come from. You want it, you buy it. Otherwise get the hell out of here."

On a sudden impulse, she reached for her wallet. Most of the time vendors didn't care if you took an hour going through everything in the booth, but Stoneman had a nasty temper, even when he wasn't drunk. She wasn't going to find out anything here. Maybe the cops should have the little paperweight, but the nearest pay phone was several rows over. If Stoneman thought the cat meant trouble, it would be gone as soon as Alice left the booth.

"I'll buy it." She didn't even haggle, paying the marked price and demanding a receipt. As she tucked it into her purse, she felt eyes on her. She looked up and saw Steve staring right at her.

TWELVE

Before Alice could react, she heard her name called. Turning her head, she saw Ryan coming in on the other side of the booth. He joined her, with a quick hug that brought a smirk from Stoneman. Glancing around, she saw Steve glaring furiously at Ryan. She turned her back. A few moments later, when she and Ryan left the stall, Steve was gone. She wondered if he had seen the crystal cat.

As they walked down the cross row, Alice could feel Stoneman's eyes following them. He was widely rumored to deal in stolen goods, but involvement in a murder was something else. If he knew where the cat came from, no wonder he had been tight-lipped. She held firmly onto her purse. That piece of glass might be the only clue to finding out the truth. And getting her scholarship back.

"Your dad said Steve was bugging you. That's not exactly how he put it, but that's how it sounded to me. What's he doing hanging around?" Ryan's arm tightened around her waist. Evidently, he hadn't seen Steve staring at them. Alice was glad; the last thing she needed was a confrontation.

"Just going on about how no one believes I don't know anything, and how much he wants to help me. Don't worry about it. I ignore him."

"According to your dad, ignoring isn't what you were doing. He said you were yelling." Ryan grinned. "Actually, I wish I could have been around to help you ignore him. I bet we could have ignored him right out of here." He lost his grin. "But I don't like him hanging around."

Alice saw some handworked silver and stopped. "Dad likes him, Ryan." She sneaked a quick peek back toward Stoneman's stall. Steve and Stoneman were having a heated discussion. For some reason the sight left her queasy. "Besides, he helps Dad with business." As she spoke, she was examining a silver bracelet closely. Inferior, sloppy work. She put it back, looking down the row of stands. Stoneman was now talking to an older couple. Steve had vanished.

"Yeah, well, he can talk to your father without having to talk to you." He looked at the gaudy ring she was holding. "Do you want that thing?"

She dropped it back on the counter. "Are you kidding? Dad could do better than that sound asleep." She smiled and shook her head at the approaching dealer. "Just looking, thanks." They moved on, heading toward her father's stand.

When they got to the truck, they had to wait several minutes while her dad finished a sale. When the lady finally left, Ryan and Alice joined Mr. Fleming. He was jubilant. One glance in the glass case told Alice why.

"Dad! The squash blossom?"

"Yep." The ornate turquoise necklace was missing from the glass case. She hugged her dad, who was grinning from ear to ear. It was his most expensive piece.

After a few minutes of rejoicing, she told him about the rock hound one row over. She and Ryan stayed while her dad made a quick run over to see if there was anything he could use. This time he'd be able to dicker without worrying about the money.

"That's wild." Ryan looked down at the display. He'd seen it before, of course, but he'd never been around when they'd had a major sale. "How much did he get for that thing, anyway?"

Alice told him. "Of course, squash blossoms are always expensive, just because there's so much turquoise and silver and work in them." She was as pleased as her dad. Ryan was still puzzled. In his family, a few hundred more or less meant nothing.

In less than a half hour, her father returned with some new stones: fire agate, some low-quality turquoise, a few rough peridots. Pleased by the sale and the new rocks, he made no objections when Alice left with Ryan.

The rest of the day was the first time Alice had really relaxed since Nancy's death. They drove through Pueblo toward the mountains, up to where they could feel the nip of the oncoming winter. The chill air of the high elevation cleared the cobwebs from her mind. By tacit agreement, any mention of baby-sitting or burglaries or murder—or especially of Steve—had been left behind on the road. All that existed was blue sky and crisp air and the mountains. And the two of them.

Alice was happy as they headed back home.

They really hadn't done anything extraordinary, but it had been a great afternoon. By the time they reached the outskirts of town it was already dark.

Instead of heading to her house, Ryan went on through town to Geponi's. The pizza parlor was always crowded on Saturday night. Twice a month, a band was hired, and most of the teenaged population of Anslow showed up to dance and consume dozens of pizzas and gallons of soft drinks.

When Alice and Ryan got to Geponi's, Rita and Eddie already had a table and a large pepperoni pizza. While Ryan went up to the counter to get them drinks, Alice sat down.

Rita slid over to make room. "We thought you weren't coming." She grinned at Alice over a slice of the pizza. Over half of it was gone. "So we waited."

"Yeah, right." Alice helped herself to a slice and reached for the crushed red pepper flakes. "How long do you think it would have taken you to have finished it?"

Eddie also took a piece. "Oh, I figure if you guys had been about another fifteen minutes we would have had it all taken care of. It's not our fault, though; Mr. G's kinda slow tonight. Go make out or something for a while, give us a chance to make up for lost time."

"Hey, big brother's a fast operator, Eddie. Wouldn't have made any difference."

Alice could feel herself blushing and fought her normal head-ducking reflex. She'd been fighting to break herself of the habit. But it wasn't easy. Especially since Eddie seemed to enjoy triggering it so much.

"Hey, Alice, you're the same color as the pizza." He picked a piece of pepperoni off the last slice and looked at the cheese-free sauce. Then he held it up critically. "Yep. Exact same color."

A cup plopped down in front of her as Ryan took a seat next to Eddie. "What's the exact same color? And who ate all the pizza!" Everyone laughed, Rita choking slightly on a mouthful of cheese.

Eddie repeated the comparison process while Alice pounded on Rita's back. "When Alice blushes, she turns the color of pizza sauce. Check it out yourself. With the new pizza you're going to order." He ducked Ryan's swing at his head and grinned. "Hey, you want more, you get to order."

Ryan stood up and headed back to the counter. As he was returning with the second pizza, the band began to play. Anguish was a popular band among the local kids and occasionally managed to get a gig in Pueblo. Alice knew the band members, as did everyone else in the room. When they weren't Anguish, two of them were in her class, and the other two had graduated the year before. The noise level quickly doubled in the restaurant. Half the kids in town were already there when Liz came in with Mike Cordova. Alice hadn't known they were dating.

She'd had enough pizza by this time, at least for a while. She nudged Rita and they headed for the ladies' room. Rita shrieked at the sight of her hair and searched through her purse for a brush. She started re-doing it as Alice dug for her lipstick. That was the problem with big purses. You could carry a lot of junk, but you were always losing things. She started pulling things out and balancing them on the back of the sink, hunting for the lipstick. She finally found it, after she'd unloaded half the contents of the bag. She started to shovel everything back in, when Rita reached out and picked up the crystal cat. She held the cat up to the light. Alice finished re-loading her purse and started to apply her lipstick.

"Where'd you get this?"

"Lea ircus." She finished her lips and repeated more clearly, "Flea Circus. I thought it was pretty." She didn't intend to tell anyone yet where she'd last seen it, or that she thought it might be a clue to the real criminals. She tucked the lipstick back into her purse and held out her hand for the small paperweight. "Let's get back to the guys."

Rita was still looking at the crystal. "Neat. I didn't know they had stuff like this at flea markets. You're right, it's pretty. I want to show Eddie." She stepped back out of the way of a trio of girls pushing in. "This place is a zoo. Let's get back before they decide we got lost."

She went out, still holding the cat. Alice was a bit uneasy at having it on public display, but Stoneman's booth had been a public place as well. She thought, *Right, next I'll be thinking I'm Nancy Drew. I have a clue, big deal.* Still, she wished Rita hadn't picked it up.

But it was too late. Rita handed it to Eddie as soon as she sat down. "Look what Alice picked up today. I thought you said they didn't have anything but junk at the Flea Circus."

"Hey, this isn't?"

"Of course it isn't. It's pretty." Eddie groaned and passed it to Ryan. Rita got it back from him and polished the pizza fingerprints off with a paper napkin. "Don't, you'll get it all greasy. It's a very original little cat. Okay, so it isn't valuable, but it's nice."

She and Eddie started squabbling in a mock fight, Rita now contending that maybe Alice wasn't wasting her time at the flea markets, and Eddie countering with cracks about the dump. It was funny, but Alice didn't like it. Even Rita's defense had an undertone she didn't appreciate, although she'd heard it before. She stood up and hauled Ryan away to the tiny dance floor, now completely jammed with sweaty bodies.

Soon Rita and Eddie were dancing as well. Alice looked back toward the table. The cat sat there in a heap of crumpled paper napkins and crushed soda cups, sparkling in the dim light.

As Anguish shifted to a slower number and she moved into Ryan's arms, Alice saw Steve standing at the end pick-up counter. Their eyes met, as he watched the dancers. She glared back for a moment, then looked up at Ryan. They started to dance and she snuggled even closer to him, deciding if Steve objected that was his problem. She had had enough of Mr. Steven Ferris for one day. When she glanced back, he was gone.

With the lack of space in Geponi's and the

noise of the band and the kids, it was easy to lose track of time. No one was shunning Alice as an outcast; there wasn't room. Several people who'd avoided her the previous week at school actually spoke to her normally. *Pizza peace treaty,* she thought giddily. Maybe all the world needs is for its leaders to be crowded together into a pizza parlor.

She didn't remember the grim realities of her present life until after they had left Geponi's and Eddie and Ryan had raced down the lake road. Eddie beat them to the lake, then he and Rita drove off with a roar and a blare of the car horn. The parking area was almost as full as it would be during daylight hours in the summer.

Ryan was laughing at Eddie's horn fanfare when she suddenly remembered.

"The cat! Ryan, we have to go back to Geponi's!"

"Now?" His arm had gone around her, pulling her close.

"Please, Ryan. I left it there."

"Can't you get it tomorrow?" He tried to hold onto her, as she pulled back. "Oh, for . . . all right, all right. I don't see why it couldn't wait." He started the car up with a roar to rival Eddie's.

When they got to Geponi's, the CLOSED

sign was on the door and the shades were drawn, but Alice could still see people moving inside. After she rapped on the glass for several minutes, Mr. Geponi opened the door.

"Sorry, we're closed. Open again at noon." He started to close the door again, but Alice blocked it with her foot.

"We were here earlier, and I left something. Can we come in and look for it?"

He thought for a moment, staring hard at Ryan as though weighing their potential as a modern day Bonnie and Clyde. Finally, he held the door open enough for them to come in.

Ryan lingered by the counter, while Alice dashed across to their table. It was useless, as she had seen as soon as they walked in. Except for the napkins holder and the little wire rack with sugar, salt, and pepper, the table was bare. Even the red pepper flakes and Parmesan were gone. The nightly cleanup was underway and a busboy was pushing a broom around the dance floor. Alice bent down to look under the table, but it had already been swept. The crystal cat had disappeared.

After some fruitless questions, they left. Alice berated herself mentally for not reclaiming the paperweight from Rita. Steve had been in Geponi's earlier, and she was sure he'd seen her buying the cat from Mr. Stoneman. Alice felt queasy, thinking of the full implications of that. She had broken up with Steve, sure, but he had been a friend most of her life. Her suspicions were hardening, and she didn't like them.

When Alice got home, both her parents were waiting up for her. That usually never happened. Her mother's lips were almost invisible, her mouth was pursed so tightly. Her father looked equally upset; all trace of the euphoria from his big sale had vanished. Dismayed, she looked at the time. It was just after midnight. She'd been out much later on Saturdays before, but she wasn't sure if she'd told Dad about going to Geponi's. She should have called. Before she could try to explain, her mother spoke.

"The police were here."

Alice's stomach suddenly regretted the earlier pizza and pepper flakes. It wasn't just a question of not calling in; there was serious trouble.

"Some of the loot from these burglaries showed up at the Flea Circus." Her mother went on. "The police were there today."

"They showed up about two hours after you and Ryan took off," her father said. "Sweetheart, I don't want to call you a liar. We talked about it this morning, on the way there. But dammit, something has to give! You haven't asked where the stuff showed up."

She shook her head, weakly. Oh no. Not . . .

"Stoneman's stall. And you were seen there today. He said you bought something, he wouldn't say what." Alice started to reach for her purse, but stopped with her hand halfway in. There was nothing left to show them.

"What makes it really bad is he had a lot of *my* stuff there as well. Jewelry you sold him last month. He said he couldn't remember when he bought anything. And he wasn't sure if you sold him any other stuff besides the jewelry or not."

As Alice shook her head violently, he sighed. "Don't you see, sweetheart? It's one more reason for the police to think you did it."

"And for you to think so?" Her voice was low and she was almost holding her breath for the answer. He sighed again.

"We don't know what to think that, Alice. We want to believe you."

"Dear, we *do* want to," her mother added. "But so far, what you've said hasn't made much sense."

"All I've said is that I don't know *anything!*"

"And that's what doesn't make sense." She spoke sadly. "There has to be a connection.

What we think, your father and I, is that maybe you told someone a few things. Maybe you don't think whoever it was could commit such horrible crimes. Well, think about this. If this person is innocent, he should come forward and tell the police. No real friend would leave you to face them alone."

"Mom, do you mean Ryan? Well, he's a real friend, and he didn't have anything to do with it. And I don't either!"

Her mom sighed and stood up. "Not just Ryan. Anybody you know. Please, Alice, think about it. For now, let's all just go to bed."

It had been a good day for the most part. But the sick feeling and the terror were back. And the nightmares. All night long, Alice dreamt she was a cat made out of crystal. She was in a giant box, and there was no way out.

THIRTEEN

Sunday dawned as bright and warm as Saturday, but the weather inside the Fleming house was anything but sunny. Winter had set in, at least judging by the way Alice's parents were acting. What made it harder was that, for the first time, Alice really was holding something back. She hadn't told her parents about the paperweight. Belatedly, it occurred to her that having one of the missing items from the murder scene wouldn't have improved her position with the police. How could she explain why she'd wanted it, without admitting she knew where it came from? And would Higgins believe her if she did tell him?

Her mother had asked what she'd bought. It was after Alice said it was a trinket she'd already lost, which was true but incomplete, that the internal climate shifted to the Ice Age. She'd never been able to lie successfully to her mother. Alice didn't know if it was her tendency to blush that gave her away, or if her mother was just psychic.

Sticking around for a day of deep freeze held little appeal. Alice called Ryan's house, hoping for some of the summer warmth of the previous day. He wasn't there, but Rita was.

"Ryan's out with Eddie, Alice, but come over anyway," Rita said, sounding tired. At Geponi's, she had been full of life and fun. Maybe it was the murder, Alice thought. It kept coming back to haunt them all.

"Sure. Can you come pick me up?" Even a gloomy Rita would be better than the tension at home.

"Alice, I'm sorry, but could you just get over here on your own? I'll explain later." There was more than fatigue in Rita's voice now; she sounded quietly frantic.

Alice had problems of her own, but that sounded like a call for help. She couldn't let Rita down. She went to get her bike. Recently it hadn't gotten much use, but it had always been her basic transportation.

When Alice got to Rita's house the reason for

the desperation was instantly obvious. Rita was on the sun deck with Liz, sitting on the long built-in couch under the south windows. Lately Liz had been acting even more strangely. Privately, Alice was amazed Rita had put up with it for the past week. Liz might be Rita's oldest friend, but she was pushing the limits of friendship awfully hard.

"Hey, the Flea Market Queen! Hi, Alice, buy any good junk yesterday?" Liz's smile was half sneer.

Alice sat down in the white wicker rocking chair. "I just rode there with my dad. Ryan and I went on from there." She had the satisfaction of seeing Liz react to that. "Sorry. If I'd known you wanted some junk, I would have stuck around longer and gotten some for you."

"No junk?" Liz raised an eyebrow. "I'm disappointed."

Alice thought of the crystal cat. She couldn't decide if Liz was hinting about it or not. Rita could have told her, but Alice wasn't going to mention it first. After all, the cat wasn't junk.

Rita echoed this, without mentioning the paperweight directly. "They have lots of real junk there, but there's some decent stuff as well."

"I suppose so. After all, *some* of the stuff that got ripped off had to be worth something. I hear that's where it's been turning up." She turned toward Alice, cocking her head to one side in a parody of friendly curiosity. "Didn't you say a flea market was a good place for people to make some fast cash? And no questions asked—that must be nice."

Alice could feel herself flushing. Liz had been making cracks all week, but this was too much. "Just what's that supposed to mean?"

"Whatever you think it means, Alice." Liz's eyes flashed malice. "You're the one that always seems to want cash, you tell me."

"Nice seeing you, Rita." Alice stood up. "Tell Ryan I was over." She didn't intend to be a target for Liz's envy darts any longer. She went back through the living room, heading for the front door. Rita hurried after her, apologizing. Behind her, she heard Liz laughing hysterically.

Just as she reached the door, it opened and Ryan almost walked over her. Alice let out a gasp of surprise, which turned to a sigh of relief as Ryan scooped her into his arms and gave her a long hug. She felt eyes on her, and looked over Ryan's shoulder. Eddie was standing there and behind him, Steve was framed in the doorway. His rattletrap Plymouth stood in the driveway. Alice stiffened. What was he doing here?

"Hey, babe. When'd you get here?" Ryan released her and they went on into the living room. Eddie had an arm around Rita's waist, as she talked to him in a low voice. An ugly scowl twisted his face, one that found focus as Liz walked into the room.

"Well, well, it's a party and nobody told me." She smiled around at everyone, her eyes glittering slightly. "But Stevie! I never expected to see you here." The emphasis on the last words were shaded just enough to make the full meaning clear to everyone: *And you're definitely not welcome.*

"Hi, Liz." Steve's greeting was flat and quiet. "Just gave Ryan and Eddie a lift."

"Yeah, the 'Vette got a flat." Eddie growled. "Steve stopped to give us a hand, and we got the lug nuts loose, then we found out the damned spare was flat as well."

"I could go get my car and give you a ride back there, Eddie," Liz offered. She was acting arch, flirtatious, and completely unnatural. Alice looked at her more closely, trying to figure out what was going on.

"I'll get my own rides, Liz." Eddie's voice was light, almost amused, but Alice shivered, remembering his rage a week ago at the lake. Possibly Liz did as well, because she turned to Steve and took his arm.

"Stevie, you can teach me all about flea markets. Is there one today? You can take me and teach me all-l-l-l about it. Never know what I might find. Or find out."

"Liz, cut it out," Ryan ordered. "You're acting like an idiot."

"Oh, I'm not an idiot. I know a few people who are, though. Maybe Stevie can explain fools and idiots to me along with flea markets?" She hung onto his arm. Alice was embarrassed for him. She knew how much he hated that nickname. No one had called him Stevie since third grade and gotten away with it.

Amazingly, he didn't shake Liz off. He didn't even say anything about the detested little-boy version of his name. He just said, "How about if I drop you off at your house instead?" They left, Liz clinging as though she needed him for a crutch.

"Wow." Rita let out a shaky laugh that sounded almost like a sob. "I think she's flipped."

"Yeah, a long time ago." Eddie looked enraged.

They went out to the back yard. Despite the departure of Liz and Steve, there was tension in the air. Rita was arguing with Eddie in a tight whisper. Alice kept an eye on them, while trying to figure out what it was that bothered her so much about Liz.

"Alice, couldn't you tell?" Ryan's voice cut across her thoughts. "She was completely bombed. That's what I meant, telling her not to be an idiot. She's been drinking a lot lately."

Alice was fitting together more puzzling bits of Liz's recent behavior. She couldn't believe she'd been so naive, but it hadn't even crossed her mind. No wonder Rita had seemed embarrassed by her friend so often. The surprise was that she hadn't dropped Liz a long time ago.

A short time later, Ryan suggested they take a drive. Getting away from Rita and Eddie sounded like a great idea to Alice, but she'd come on her bike. They'd have to put it in the back seat. She went to bring it around to the car.

She rolled the bike up the driveway toward the garage, along the solid wood fence. As she reached Ryan's convertible, she heard him talking to Eddie in the back yard. Talking wasn't quite the right word. They were yelling at each other.

". . . do what I want to."

"Eddie, I'm not saying it again. You do, you'll regret it. I think you'd better think it over real hard and change your mind about a few things, because I'm not going to put up with much more. You got it?"

A moment later, the tall gate in the fence banged open, swinging all the way flat against the fence. Ryan paused, seeing her, then came over and hoisted the bike into the car. Alice went around and got in, as he started the car.

"You hear any of that?"

"A little. Ryan, what's wrong? Is it just because Liz has everyone on edge, or what?"

He relaxed his white-knuckle grip on the wheel slightly. "Yeah, Liz is part of it. I think she's getting way out of control, but Rita doesn't want to drop her. I think she feels sorry for her. And Eddie . . . let's just say he's about had it with Liz himself. I just don't want him and Rita fighting, is all. I don't want her hurt. And I've been a little worried about her. Eddie better not make her unhappy."

The last part was spoken so quietly it was almost to himself. Alice didn't think Ryan was really talking to her as much as he was still arguing with Eddie. All of the hassles had her brooding again on her own fears. She spoke as much to herself as Ryan had just done.

"I wish I weren't so unhappy myself."

Ryan pulled over and stopped. Unbuckling his seatbelt, he turned toward her and took her hand. "Okay, let's have it. I know all of this stuff about the burglaries has you upset, the fact that you know the people and everything, but you sound like you're worried about a lot more than that."

"I am!" It all came pouring out: the coincidences, Higgins, the nightmares, the Flea Circus, Sam's, her terror, all in a jumbled tangle. Before she was halfway through, tears were flooding down her cheeks unheeded. Ryan had believed her all along, but she'd kept most of it bottled up inside, trying to forget it when she was with him. Telling it was an almost painful release.

". . . and then last Thursday, when the prowler almost broke in and Higgins still wouldn't believe me, that was when I knew no one ever would, and so I didn't even think about telling him when I bought . . ."

"Hold it." He cut her off. "What happened Thursday?"

"I was baby-sitting and a prowler almost got in—he broke a window—only I called 911."

"Alice. *Exactly what happened*?" He grasped her by the shoulders, his fingers digging into her flesh. She winced and he slackened his grip, but he didn't let go. With some more prodding, she managed a coherent version of the incident at the Eisens' house. When she finished, he was furious. He asked only one question.

"Why didn't you tell me?"

"I was afraid." Before he could misunderstand, she stumbled on. "I was afraid to even talk about it, Ryan. Before, I just thought it was all some horrible mistake. After that, I started thinking it was intentional. Which meant maybe Nancy was an accident, but if something happened to me, it wouldn't be." She ducked her head.

He was silent for a long time. At last she raised her own head. He was sitting still, staring straight ahead. A muscle was jumping in the side of his cheek.

"Ryan?"

He reached for the key and started the car again, pulling away from the curb jerkily. He drove on in silence. Finally he spoke.

"Alice, don't worry about it. Nothing will happen to you. I promise."

"Ryan, you can't promise me that. Right now, even Higgins couldn't. I just wish it were over."

When Alice got home, her mother told her Steve had called twice. After the earlier scene, she was happy to have missed him. She told her mother as much and went on to her room. She didn't intend to call Steve back, no matter what. But later on, after supper, he called again. Her mother insisted she take the call.

"Alice, have you seen Liz?"

"Not since the two of you left Ryan's."

"Damn. Alice, I'm worried about her."

"I'm sorry, Steve. She's got problems, but right now so do I, and since one of her favorite games is Bug Alice, I'm not too sympathetic."

"I noticed. Look, it may be more than just bugging. She's been talking kind of wild lately about a lot of things, like the burglaries and Nancy. I better find her."

"Good luck." She was ready to hang up.

"Yeah. By the way, how come you had a ringside seat for that mess today?"

The nosy question was the final straw. Her anger exploded.

"Ryan's my boyfriend, and Rita's my friend, and it is absolutely none of your business when I go to their house, or why, or how often, or anything else!"

"None of my . . . look, Alice, you seem to keep forgetting I'm still your friend, too. We've known each other all our lives. And anytime I see a friend . . ."

"I said it was none of your business," she interrupted him. "And I pick my own friends."

"Alice, I swear, I don't think you're the same girl . . ." She slammed the receiver down.

Her mother was staring at her from across the room, upset by the audible end of the conversation. She hadn't been eavesdropping; Alice's voice was at a volume that she couldn't help hearing. Her mother echoed Steve's last remark.

"Alice, I don't know what's gotten into you since the start of the school year, but the way you're acting, you don't seem like my little girl anymore."

Alice couldn't stand it. She ran out of the house, with nothing in mind except escape. Once she was outside, she started walking. It was late, but there was no school the following day. Not that she would have cared if there was. Not now.

She walked for hours, finally coming home exhausted. The house was quiet. She slipped into her room, falling at once into a dreamless sleep.

FOURTEEN

When Alice's mother came in shortly after nine and shook her lightly, Alice rolled over and tried to go back to sleep. Mumbling into her pillow, she said, "Go 'way. No school t'day, lemme sleep." A faculty workshop meant there would be no school for two days.

"Alice, wake up, honey. Please, you have to wake up."

Something in her mother's voice cut through the fog. She sounded upset. Upset and trying not to show it. Alice twisted her head around to look at her. One glimpse of her mother's ashen face and she rolled over and sat up in one movement.

"Mom, what's wrong? Why aren't you at work?" A horrible thought hit. "Is something wrong with Dad?"

"No, he's fine." Her mom shook her head. "I told you yesterday I wasn't going in till noon. No, that's not the problem."

Alice swung her feet off the bed. "Then what is?"

"You'd better get dressed quickly and come down to the living room. Detective Higgins is here again and he wants to ask you some more questions."

"Now? They must have found some more stuff."

Her mother gave a hopeless shrug.

Alice stood up and headed for the bathroom. She stopped halfway and turned back. "Tell him I'll be out in a few minutes. Mom, it's okay. It really is. I didn't do anything, and I am the same person I was a month ago."

Mom looked around the bedroom, as though to reassure herself on that point. Her eyes lingered for a moment on the stack of college catalogs on the end of the bookshelf. Alice added, "It'll all get sorted out pretty soon, I'm sure." With the confident assurance went a voiceless prayer. *Please let it be over soon.*

"I hope so, Alice."

Higgins's eyes fastened on Alice as she entered the living room and sat down next to her mother. When he had urged her to come clean, there had been traces of compassion and sympathy in his expression. Now there were none. His face was expressionless, and his eyes were cold and hard. The same uniformed officer sat in the big chair, as silent as before, notebook ready.

"Mrs. Fleming. Would you like to call your husband at work?" Even when speaking to her mother, his eyes never left Alice. "We could wait for him, if you wished. Or for an attorney. If you can't afford an attorney, we could call the public defender's office."

Her mother was unable to control a slight gasp at this, but she answered steadily enough. "No, Detective Higgins, we'll be fine on our own. Alice has told us she has nothing to do with these crimes and we believe her."

Alice squeezed her hand, fighting the sting of tears. She knew her parents did in fact have doubts, which made this support all the more welcome. Any uncertainty she might have had about their faith in her had vanished. It meant a lot.

"Ms. Fleming." He went on, ignoring her mother and focusing solely on Alice. He wasn't calling her Alice today, she noticed. "You have the right to remain silent. You have . . ."

He went on giving her the Miranda rights, so

familiar from years of TV. She sat stunned. Miranda rights were usually given just before an arrest! Her grip on her mother's hand tightened. She felt as though that grip was the only solid point left in the universe.

When he finished, she shook her head again. She didn't want to get cluttered up with a lawyer, but from the sound of things, she would need one soon. Maybe her cooperative attitude would count in her favor.

"No lawyers. I'll tell you anything I can." She stressed the last word.

Higgins started the questioning abruptly. "Do you know a Ms. Elizabeth Hamilton? When did you see her last?"

Liz? Alice answered promptly and with no reservations. "Yes, I know Liz. I saw her yesterday afternoon at Rita and Ryan's house. The Derosas. She left at, oh, about four-thirty. With Steve. That's Steve Ferris—he was here when you questioned me the first time."

"Did she seem normal?"

Alice's determination to tell everything foundered. Liz was underage, and Alice didn't like gossiping. Her mother seemed to sense her doubt and gave her hand the slightest squeeze. It was a reminder of her parents' faith in her. So be it; she'd go ahead and tell Higgins everything.

"She was acting kind of weird. Ryan said she had been drinking. I think she has a problem with it."

The questioning went on, about Liz's drinking, how close they were, her recent behavior, and several other tacks that seemed strange. Why didn't he just ask Liz? Alice was beginning to think there was something peculiar about this. Liz was in trouble; Higgins must suspect her. While Alice didn't really think Liz could be involved, she knew *she* wasn't. And it would be a relief for the attention to be focused elsewhere.

Then, abruptly, Higgins shifted the spotlight back onto her. "Ms. Fleming, how long have you been planning to go to Colorado College? Haven't you said you were going, and I quote, 'come hell or high water'? Haven't you expressed a strong desire for money many times, to many people, to reach this goal?"

"Yes I have." Alice felt the stirring of anger. "I'm not the only person who's ever said things like that. All of a sudden, I'm a criminal because I was determined."

"No, Ms. Fleming. Not a criminal for being determined." He stood up, signaling his silent

167

partner with his eyes. The uniformed man closed the notebook and slid it into his pocket. "Not for wanting to go to college. But maybe for the way you chose to go about it."

For a moment, anger and relief both left her speechless. Apparently she was not going to be arrested, but she was tired of innuendo. "What happened, anyway? Something must have. Why all the questions about Liz? How come you don't just ask her?"

"Mrs. Fleming, we'll be in touch. Please make sure your daughter remains within this jurisdiction. You and your husband might want to give serious consideration to retaining a lawyer."

"What happened?" Alice almost shouted the question.

Higgins looked at her, his eyes still cold and hard. Several long moments passed in total silence.

"Elizabeth Hamilton's body was found this morning near the old boathouse at Reiker's Lake," he answered quietly. "This time, it wasn't a case of burglars breaking in and panicking. This was deliberate. She was murdered."

He closed the door, quite gently. Alice and her mother sat frozen. Then with a convulsive shudder, the paralysis broke in a flood of tears. Her mother wrapped her arms around her as though Alice were a tiny child again, and rocked her back and forth. As the storm subsided, Mrs. Fleming stood.

"I'm calling your father. Sweetheart, no matter what, we're your parents and we love you. We have to find out what's going on. Two people are dead, Alice. I don't want the third one to be you."

She went to phone Alice's father, while Alice sat on the end of the couch, shivering. She hadn't known Nancy except as a face in the halls at school, a picture in the yearbook. But Liz was close. Even if she didn't get along with her all the time, she was part of the same group, and she was someone Alice knew pretty well.

Although perhaps she hadn't known Liz as well as she thought. Alice pictured Liz as she'd been the day before, her bright yellow blouse and sour smile, the cutting edge to her voice. Ryan's words about Liz's drinking came back to her. She'd been drinking more and more often, he'd said, in larger and larger quantities. What had Liz been hiding? She'd been hinting around about Nancy and the burglaries, Steve said. What had she known?

Alice wondered aloud about it to her parents a half hour later. Her dad brushed it aside.

"Alice, we have no way of knowing that, but it should convince you to figure out how you're involved."

He sighed. "We've been through this whole subject before too many times. But it was one thing when we were just worried about you being charged with a crime. Now we're worried about you getting killed. I doubt if Liz thought she'd be murdered. So I want you to think long and hard about what you might know. I don't want the killer figuring you're a threat as well."

He stopped, then without another word he and her mother left the room. Alice still sat there shivering. Only a few weeks before, she'd been heading for a fairy-tale ending. Even if there was no such thing as Happily Ever After, she thought her college goals would be achieved. Now she was stuck in an unending nightmare instead.

The phone rang, startling her. The ugly mental images of Liz's dead body faded slightly as she reached for it.

"Hello, Alice? This is Mrs. Komax. Dear, I'm afraid I have some bad news for you . . ." It was unfair for such bad news to come from such a nice source, Alice thought wildly, as the final nails went into the coffin of her dreams. The city council was requesting that her name be withdrawn from consideration for the scholarship.

She listened, almost beyond shock now. Mrs. Komax didn't mention Liz, so Alice didn't either. She wasn't sure if the news was out yet or not; Higgins hadn't said. Numbly she thanked Mrs. Komax for letting her know so quickly. Not that it made any difference whether she found out now or next week. But the council probably would announce it right away, distancing themselves and the town from Alice.

Even though it would mean talking about Liz, Alice decided to call Rita. Alice had known Liz for a short while, but Liz had been close to Rita since kindergarten.

"Rita? Have you heard . . ." The question was unnecessary. The wild sobs on the phone told their own story.

A different voice came on the phone. She heard Ryan tell Rita, "Go lie down," then he said, "Hello?" His voice was more lifeless than Alice had ever heard it.

"Ryan? What happened to Liz?"

There wasn't much to know, but the little there was he shared. A jogger had found the body early that morning. As with Nancy, someone had bashed her head in. It looked as though it had been done the night before. Rita had been crying all morning, and their doctor had been over to give her tranquilizers. When Alice told him about her morning, and the visit from Higgins, he was horrified afresh. The cancellation of the scholarship was bad enough, but he was appalled by the questioning.

"Why? For God's sake, Alice, you were home with your parents last night! I was thinking the only good thing might be the police leaving you alone on this."

"After supper, I got upset about something, and I went out. I walked for hours, Ryan, just thinking. And I didn't see anyone, I kept on quiet streets. I didn't know I was going to need an alibi."

"Alice, I still don't think they could . . ."

"Look, at this point I don't think it would matter if I had the entire Anslow City Council as an alibi. Higgins wouldn't believe them. I don't know if he thinks I killed Liz myself, or just helped someone, but he's made up his mind I'm part of it."

"Damn. Why couldn't you have been out with your parents or something?"

"I hope you and Rita have alibis at least."

She intended it to be a light comment, but it fell flat.

"We rented some videos and stayed in. I guess they might remember me at the store. Yeah, we have an alibi. I just wish you did."

Her thoughts returned grimly to her last glimpse of Liz, the day before. She had been leaning on Steve's arm, laughing, saying she would make Steve teach her about flea markets. He was an old friend, and the thought that came to mind wasn't very nice. But she voiced it anyway.

"I wonder if Steve has one."

FIFTEEN

A few hours later Alice had the chance to question Steve herself, but she hesitated to do so. She was sitting at the kitchen table, trying to decide if it was even worth asking the city council to reconsider, when he knocked. She looked up and saw him through the glass. He came in before she could say anything. She thought about what she'd said to Ryan. But murderer or not, it wasn't easy asking for an alibi from someone you remembered from kindergarten. Steve brought the subject up himself within the first few minutes. He dropped into the chair beside her and spoke abruptly.

"I was right to worry about Liz last night. I knew she was in trouble and heading for more, but I didn't know it was that bad. Why the little fool didn't. . . . My folks weren't home last night, and I was out cruising around, looking for her. Where were you? With Ryan?"

She shook her head. "I was out walking. Alone."

"Great. Just great. You and your precious Ryan . . . only good thing about this is I think you've gotten caught in your own trap this time, Alice. I don't know how you thought you could splash mud on me and keep your hands clean, but it hasn't worked. Sure, you got me into it, but you're in just as deep as I am."

"Huh?" She had no idea what he was talking about, but he was sounding rougher, more angry, than she'd ever heard him. Before he could go on, her mother poked her head in.

"Who . . . oh, it's you, Steve. Hello." Her mom smiled at them both, seemingly oblivious to the tension crackling through the kitchen. "I thought I heard voices. Alice, I'll be out in the garden if anyone calls." Obviously, her mother was trying to make everything seem normal. Alice waited until she heard the door to the back porch shut before she spoke again.

"What are you talking about? Yeah, I'm in deep—tell me something I don't know. You'll be happy to hear they canceled the scholarship, you seem to be so eager to see me get hurt. I don't know anything about you being in trouble, though. I haven't heard of the cops going after anyone except me."

"I'm not happy about you being in trouble, Alice." His face hardened. "I wish you'd never gotten so messed up in the first place. But you didn't have to drag me into it as well. Since you did, I'm not going to pretend I'm unhappy about your little problems."

"Little problems!"

"Yeah, little. Losing a scholarship isn't half as bad as what Liz lost. Or as bad as going to jail for years. They're going to try whoever it is as an adult. They can do that, you know. I may wind up in the state penitentiary. You may be going to prison instead of college. You like that idea?"

Prison. He was just trying to scare her. "Steve, you're out of your mind. I didn't do anything, I'm not going to go to prison! If you did something, then maybe you will, but *I didn't!*"

"That's not what those cops seemed to think. The ones that were all over me this morning."

"They were asking *you* questions?" Alice wondered if any new evidence had been found, and if so how long it would take them to come after her.

"Yeah, all morning. As if you didn't know.

They had a tip, they said." Steve smiled, a sour expression that wasn't pleasant to look at. "They seemed to expect to find something, but they didn't have much luck."

"So why are you bugging me about it?" Alice didn't like the way he was looking at her, waiting for some reaction. "I don't know why you're acting as if it's my fault you're in trouble."

"If it isn't you, it's that precious boyfriend of yours. You really like how he's used you? How he's used me? If it wasn't you who told the police about the pawnshops I deal with, who was it?"

"Pawnshops?" The sudden shift caught her off balance.

"Yeah, somebody gave the cops a list of just about every pawnshop and secondhand store in the state I've ever set foot in and told them to check for the stolen goods. And guess what they've been turning up! And someone also told them I'm more money-hungry than you are, evidently. That part doesn't sound like you, I admit. I've never heard you call yourself money-hungry. I think that may have come from Liz— it sounds like her style. But someone put her up to it. And now she can't tell us who it was. I don't think that's a coincidence."

"Why would I tell the police I was after

money? Or have Liz tell them?" Steve wasn't even telling a logical story.

"I don't think you would." His grin was nasty. "I think you've just been given a peek at what the Derosas really think of people like you and me. Ryan needs to get the cops on me. He'll throw you to the wolves as well. Or maybe Liz just improvised that part, and he got mad at her. Not that it's going to help you any."

He leaned back in his chair, feigning a sudden nonchalance. "No, Alice, my love, you and I are a team as far as the police are concerned. We planned it all together—for the money. You arranged for the Raineys' house to be empty. Just a tragic accident that they hired Nancy at the last minute." He leaned even further back, balancing the chair on its rear legs. "And Liz was starting to talk, so we killed her. And all because you wanted money to go to a fancy school and I wanted money for hardware. But as far as the cops are concerned, we're a couple. A couple of crooks and killers."

"I thought you said they were questioning you," Alice snapped. "Not telling you their theories."

"Yeah, well, when they kept asking me how much my girlfriend knew about the murder . . . girlfriend meaning you . . ."

"I'd sooner date a rattlesnake."

He dropped the chair back to all fours with a crash and leaned forward. His right hand plunged into his pocket, and for a wild instant Alice expected him to pull out a gun. What came out was almost as startling.

He held the crystal cat up to the light. She gasped and snatched for it, but he held it out of reach. "If you don't want to be linked with me, you better tell your spoiled brat boyfriend to stop framing me." He looked at it again, almost as though it was a fortune-teller's crystal ball, then dropped it on the table.

"Where did you get this!" she demanded fiercely, snatching it up. All the suspicions seething in her mind solidified around Steve, focused there by the cat, like sunlight through the crystal. She remembered how he had glared at her at Geponi's the night the cat disappeared.

"Surprised to see it? Maybe surprised I wasn't arrested? I damned near was. But the frame doesn't fit, Alice—you'll have to try another size."

"Where did you find it?" The words came out tightly, the effort of not screaming straining her voice.

"I found it right where your boyfriend," he almost spat the word out, "left it. In my car, wedged down between the seats. I found it; the cops didn't. Lucky for me I dropped my keys down there. I fished it out not more than half an hour before the cops showed up. I figured it didn't hurt to let them search my car, since this thing was in my mom's jewelry box by then. I never figured you'd actually try to frame me, Alice." There was hurt in his voice, but it was almost completely obscured by rage.

"I didn't." None of this was making sense to Alice at all. "Why would I?"

"The cops had already talked to that old goat out at the Flea Circus. Stoneman told them he sold the thing to someone but he didn't know who."

"He sold it to me." She felt a wash of thankfulness for having insisted on that receipt. She'd give it to her mother for safe keeping. It might be important to be able to prove she'd bought it legally. "When did you steal it back? From the table at Geponi's that night? Or did Liz steal it then? Did you take it back after you killed her?"

She had no idea she was going to say that until the words left her mouth. He froze for a moment, then staggered to his feet, swearing at her. His fists clenched, and she shrank back away from him.

"*What in the hell do you mean?*" he shouted,

his voice cracking with intensity. An ugly flush had spread to the back of his neck, and his face was twisted and blood red.

"You did it, you must have!" She could feel the tears building, but she wouldn't let them go. "Liz must have been drunk, and Nancy was tiny and you surprised her, but right now you'd better not try anything, Steve, you really better not. I'm ready for it, and Mom's right outside. You wanted the money, so you pulled those burglaries. You tried to make it look like vandalism, but it didn't work. And you've been after me for a month to drop Ryan and start dating you again. When I didn't, you started trying to frame me, and then you tried to break in the other night at the Eisens'. Well, it didn't work, and now it's broad daylight, Steve. I'm not all alone on a baby-sitting job."

She was getting dizzy. Steve stood paralyzed against the rush of words, as though the accusations had turned him to stone. She was standing now, ready to run or fight. She wasn't going to sit quietly and let herself be murdered. Or be framed for Liz's murder.

"I wonder if you meant to kill me that first night. Did Nancy just get in the way? It must have been frustrating, not being able to get at me. I haven't done any baby-sitting since the

Eisens, and you blew it that time. It's going to be tough getting Higgins to believe me; you've done a great job of poisoning him against me. But I'm going to tell everyone, Steve, and I'm not Liz. You can't shut me up the way you did her. You can head for Mexico, or give yourself up, but it's over. I'm not going to be the scapegoat any more."

By the time she finished speaking, Steve had gone dead white. He moved toward her and she jumped back, but he didn't attack. He just continued in a straight line to the door. To it, out it, and away. The sound of his car was a signal for her to breathe. She gave way to the shakes. Oddly, there were no tears left. Perhaps this time the anger and the adrenaline had combined to burn them out of her.

She'd have to tell her parents, and get them to go with her to Higgins. Telling the detective wouldn't be that bad, but telling her folks would be. Steve had betrayed them as much as her, Alice thought. Jealousy. It was hard to believe Steve could have been that twisted by jealousy, but she couldn't think of another explanation.

She heard the bang of the garden door. By the time her mother came into the kitchen, Alice was fixing a pot of coffee. If her hands shook a little, her mother didn't comment. Instead, frowning slightly, she started with the most awkward question of all.

"Why did Steve leave in such a hurry, Alice? Have you two been fighting again?"

Alice felt her resolve crumbling like a dead leaf. She'd tell both her parents together. Later. After she told Ryan. She nodded her head, jerkily.

"That's too bad." Her mother's sigh was barely audible. "Your father left some information for him on that festival next year. If he'd waited a few minutes, I could have given it to him."

Alice felt like saying he wouldn't need it where he was going, but refrained. With a mumbled apology, she left the kitchen in a hurry. She was no good at acting a part and never had been. She couldn't believe how well Steve had managed to do it.

Once out of the kitchen, she went right to the phone. She wanted the comfort of Ryan's voice, and she didn't want to carry the weight of her suspicions alone any longer. If only Liz had said something to her and to Rita, instead of just hinting. . . . She stopped herself. *If onlys* never helped.

Rita answered the phone on the first ring.

Alice braced herself for the grief she expected. What she heard was fear.

"Alice? Oh, I'm so glad you called. Please, I've got to talk to you, it's important. Can you meet me someplace?"

"Sure, I guess. Or Ryan could pick me up. But first, can I talk to him?"

"He's not here." Rita gulped down noisy sobs. "He's . . . Alice, I think he's in danger. It's complicated. . . ."

Alice felt ice forming in her stomach. "Rita, what's happened? What danger?"

"I can't explain, honest! Look, just meet me at the turnoff to Reiker's Lake. I'll explain everything then. Only don't tell anyone where you're going. Don't even tell anyone you *are* going anyplace."

"Rita? Why . . . ?"

"I said I'll explain everything as soon as you meet me. But please, Alice, don't let anyone know. Not your mom, not anyone."

"Well . . ."

"Please!" Rita's voice was desperate. "I don't want Ryan to get hurt!"

"Neither do I." Alice decided suddenly she'd do it. "I'll meet you, but it will take a while. I'll have to ride my bike."

"Just get there as soon as you can, okay?" A click, and Rita was gone.

Alice grimly replayed the conversation in her head. Rita had sounded desperate. Concern for her twin brother was the only thing likely to hit her that hard. So Ryan was in some sort of trouble. The question was, how could Alice help by meeting Rita?

She could think of one possible explanation, and it frightened her. Steve hadn't been able to get at her here. Was he trying again? Wild visions flashed through her head. Steve holding a gun on Ryan and Rita; Steve framing Ryan; Steve threatening Rita to make Ryan write a confession. It didn't make any sense, really, but nothing about the whole situation made sense.

One thing she did understand, though, and she didn't like it one bit. For some reason, she was supposed to meet Rita without telling anyone. And at the lake turnoff. Liz had been found out at the lake. If Steve was using Rita somehow, that meant Alice was walking right into a trap if she did what Rita asked. But if she didn't?

The answer to part of the problem was right in front of her, quite literally right by her hand. Her journal. She'd been keeping a record of her senior year. She might not finish her senior year now, but she'd sure leave a record. She started writing, rapidly pouring her suspicions and hurt and sense of betrayal onto the page. If this was a setup, she'd let Steve know she'd left this on her desk. Even if he killed her, he wouldn't get away with it.

She stopped writing when she realized she'd shifted from an outline of her suspicions and what had happened to her feelings about Steve and why he would do this to her. This wasn't the time for a theme on jealousy. It would be easy to think she should never have dropped him, but that wasn't the answer. If he was that jealous, he was insane. Catering to it wouldn't have helped.

She left the journal under the rest of her textbooks. If anything happened, someone would have to go through the books, and surely someone would have enough curiosity to open her journal and read the last entry. Whoever it was would get an eyeful.

Alice hurried out, scowling at herself. She'd decided to follow Rita's instructions exactly. She hoped to get out the door unobserved, but her mother was in the kitchen, cleaning some of the last garden squash of the season. Alice swore mentally and headed for the door with a fast, "Bye, Mom." It didn't work.

"Alice? We're having dinner a little early tonight; were you going someplace?"

"Just for a bike ride, Mom." Her smile felt hideously forced, even to herself, but the events of the day were reason enough for strain. "I shouldn't be gone too long." *I hope.*

SIXTEEN

Half an hour later, she turned down the lake road. Rita's car was a few hundred feet from the highway on a pull-off. Alice parked her bike behind the trees that separated the graveled area from the fields lining the road and ran to the car. As she scrambled into the front seat, Rita started the engine. They were moving before Alice's door was even shut.

"I got here as fast as I could. Now what's wrong?"

Rita didn't answer. Alice felt the ice of fear. At least Steve wasn't here holding a gun on Rita, but it might be something just as bad. Rita wasn't capable of speech at the moment, she was sobbing too wildly. They flew around a sharp curve in the road. Alice held her breath as the car fishtailed and kept going.

"Rita, what is it? Want me to drive? *Rita!*"

A strangled sob came out around a single word, which might or might not have been "lake." Alice gritted her teeth. She wanted to shake Rita and make her explain, but until the car was stopped, it was much too dangerous. It was less than two miles to the lake; she'd have to wait. They roared down the road at seventy-five miles an hour, Rita's sobbing almost drowning the sound of the powerful engine.

When they reached the lake, it seemed for a moment to Alice that Rita would drive right into the water. With only a few feet to spare, she skidded to a stop beside the path down to the old dock. The parking lot was deserted—it was near sunset and winter was close. The nip in the air kept most people from wanting to spend time on or near the water.

Rita killed the engine, then dropped her head on her crossed arms on the steering wheel. She had progressed almost to hysteria. Alice wasn't sure how to handle this, but she had to find out what was going on.

"Rita, settle down. It's okay, you can tell me now. What's going on? Rita, answer me. *Rita . . .*"

Alice reached for Rita, intending to slap her. There was a sudden draft behind her. Almost as soon as she became aware of the cold air, a strong hand seized her arm and dragged her backwards from the car. She twisted around, trying to fight, and the words died on her lips.

Eddie had her right arm in a grip so tight each finger was outlined in white. It looked grotesque, since his hand was sheathed in a thin rubber glove. His face was a snarl of triumph and something else. Alice didn't recognize the emotion, but it terrified her. He started to drag her down the path to the old boathouse. She struggled, but he only clenched more tightly.

Behind them, Rita wailed, "I'm sorry, I'm *sorry*, oh God, Alice, I'm sorry but he said he'd kill Ryan and we didn't mean for any of this to happen and I'm *sorry*. . . ."

"Shut up!" Eddie growled. "Gutless little . . ."

He broke off and yanked at Alice. She stumbled after him, too stunned to fight anymore. She'd seen what was in his right hand. A tire iron.

Eddie saw her terrified look. "Yeah, like she says, sorry. Too bad. You can blame your friend Liz. If she'd kept her damned mouth shut, I wouldn't have to do this."

Have to do this. Suddenly she knew what the

strange look on his face was. Eddie was high and he was psyching himself up for the kill.

"Eddie." Alice fought to keep her voice steady—she didn't want to push him over the edge. "Eddie, I left a message in my journal. I figured everything out earlier and I wrote it all down. It won't do you any good to kill me now."

She cried out as his fingers bit deeper into her arm. The tire iron came up, and she tried to shrink back. It was inches from crushing her skull. "You little . . . ! Rita, dammit, shut up! You're going to have to get into her house and get that damned journal. But," he relaxed slightly, "even if we can't get it, the cops won't be able to pin this on us. They probably won't even try, with all the nice clear fingerprints I'm giving them."

She looked at the tire iron, mesmerized. Now she could see how carefully he was holding it— protecting someone's fingerprints.

"Stevie-boy's going to regret playing Good Samaritan on that flat tire. He even lent me his tire iron. You two really set yourselves up, you know that? You buying that cat, him going into Sam's and leaving prints all over those nice glass counters . . . hell, it's no wonder the cops haven't looked at me! Or at lover-boy Ryan."

Alice struggled wildly. She tried to bite his hand, but had to duck and almost fell as he brought the tire iron up again.

"What's the matter, you didn't figure out lover-boy was in it? What the hell did you put in that note?"

"Steve." The whisper was involuntary, as she realized how perfectly the frame would fit Steve now. So did Eddie, who laughed maniacally.

"I don't believe it! This is awesome. Alice, you know what?" His voice was mock solemn, his eyes were wild. He was near the edge. "I'm going to kill you, Alice. The police are going to find your poor dead body, and the tire iron, and they'll find just enough prints on it. And there's your little journal, with you accusing Stevie-boy. I'm not framing him, Alice, you are."

"Not Ryan." Steve hadn't betrayed their friendship after all. But Ryan . . . if he could do this to her, then she really had been living in Wonderland for the past month.

Eddie laughed again, but his grip didn't slacken for an instant. "It'd be fun to make you think that . . . but nah, he started wimping out when Nancy got in the way. Everything was smooth up till then." He sneered openly at Rita, who was stumbling down the path behind them. She cowered back. The reaction was automatic, as though she was used to this sort of treatment.

"Ryan will threaten me, he'll probably even cry when they find your body, but it'll be just like Liz. He might be willing to risk himself, but he won't risk baby sister. He'll keep his mouth shut. He started it all anyway."

They were getting closer to the boathouse. Alice jerked back, but she couldn't break free. Maybe she could stall him. "And Liz? Was she in it, too? What happened, did the thieves have a falling out?"

"Liz was asking for it. Talking to Steve, talking to you—hell, for all I know talking to the governor." He hefted the tire iron, almost unconsciously. "What'd she tell you?"

"She didn't tell me anything. I don't know why you think she did." She had to keep him talking, anything to keep him talking, out here in the open where there might be a chance to run. If he got her into that boathouse, it was all over.

"Don't lie to me, Alice. I want to know. She told you something, I know that. Now tell me what." He twisted her arm suddenly, viciously, and she almost fainted.

"She didn't say anything!" It was almost a shriek.

"She told me she did. She told me she'd told you everything." He wrenched her arm again. All his teeth were showing in a grimace that was not a smile. "And then I killed her."

"Liz was my best friend, and you killed her," Rita sobbed. "And now Alice . . ."

Only the fact that both his hands were full was keeping Eddie from striking Rita. "Yeah, now Alice. Shut up, or you're next. I've had enough of you and your damned guilt trips and crying anyway."

Rita hiccuped and fell silent. From the look on her face, she believed him completely. In the stillness, Alice suddenly heard a note of hope. It was the sound of a car, heading toward the lake, fast.

Eddie and Rita heard it as well. Rita scrambled back up the path, back toward the parking area, in a panic. Eddie swore viciously and pulled Alice toward the boathouse. It was only yards away. She was fighting harder than she ever could have imagined—fighting for her life. He swore again and swung at her with the tire iron, but his foreshortened blow missed. For a moment, his grip on her arm weakened, and she tore free and fled, toward the sound of the car.

She reached the edge of the parking lot and

faltered. Ryan had gotten out of his car and was heading toward her, Rita clinging to his arm. The momentary hesitation was too much; Eddie grabbed her from behind. For an instant, all four of them froze.

"Let her go, Eddie. Just let her go." Ryan was breathing hard. He controlled himself with an effort. "I told you to leave Alice out of it." Behind him, Rita had sunk to her knees, still sobbing.

Eddie pulled Alice roughly back against him. He was panting as well. She could feel the tire iron hovering inches from her head, and braced herself to duck if it descended, knowing how futile the effort would be.

"No way, Ryan. Little Alice here is our chance to get off the hook." He started pushing her forward. "Think! Steve's tire iron, Steve's prints, she even wrote about him in her diary or whatever. We shut her up and they'll nail Steve. It'll be over, we'll be done with it."

He shifted his grip. "Just turn around. Or take Rita and go back to town. This won't take long, then we set up the alibi, and we don't ever have to do another damned thing. Use your head, it's the only way out."

His left hand had Alice's arm twisted up behind her back in a steel grip. He forced her to her knees and raised the tire iron for a killing blow. She twisted desperately in his grasp. Only a few feet away, she saw Ryan start to turn his back. He was going to let Eddie kill her.

Then he shouted, "Alice, *run!*," as he whirled and launched a flying tackle at Eddie.

The blow from the tire iron went wild, ripping up a chunk of dirt and grass, as Ryan knocked Eddie off his feet. Alice was torn from his grasp and scrambled to her feet, running away without a backward glance. Behind her she could hear them fighting, and Eddie's foul cursing.

She ran across the parking lot, toward the road. The open fields lining the road offered no concealment, but on the road itself she could hope for a car, a rescue. Not that she thought it through. Safety lay in getting as far away from Eddie as she could, as fast as she could. The bare gravel road stretched toward the highway, two miles away. She ran on, her feet slipping in the gravel.

Behind her there was a sick *thud* and a piercing scream. Stumbling, she looked back over her shoulder. Ryan was collapsed in a heap on the ground, his head spurting blood. Rita clung to Eddie's arm, hampering him, keeping him from striking Ryan again. Her screams continued, mixed with words that couldn't be understood.

Alice almost fell. She looked back at the road, trying to see through the blur of tears. *Ryan* . . . He'd saved her life and he was dead.

Maybe he'd saved her life. She risked another glance. Rita was sobbing over Ryan's crumpled body. Eddie, bloody tire iron still in his hand, was sprinting for Ryan's car. He reached it and started it with a roar. He was coming after her.

The highway was too far away; he'd have her in another few minutes. She plunged forward anyway. Irrigation ditches, too wide to jump, lined the road, with barbed wire fences beyond them. Running wouldn't do any good, but if she tried to get into the fields, she'd be trapped against ditch and fence. All she could do was fight till the end.

Her breath was coming in short gasps. At least Rita was still alive, but she doubted Eddie would let her stay that way, and even if Ryan wasn't dead, he soon would be. Eddie was out of control; the temper she'd glimpsed before had finally gotten out of the cage that had been the public Eddie. First he'd catch her, then he'd go back for Rita. Her only prayer was that

Eddie would be caught later. The thought of her journal burned at her as she ran.

Suddenly she blinked hard, feeling a desperate hope. A car was coming toward her in a cloud of dust. The roar of Ryan's car behind her had masked its approach. Now the note changed, as she looked back one last time. The convertible was skidding, fishtailing violently. As Eddie wrenched into a tight turn, an old Plymouth skidded to a stop beside her.

She jumped in beside Steve. It seemed the most normal thing in the world for him to be here. Eddie headed back for the lake, and with a spurt of gravel Steve took off after him.

"Thank God. I've been looking for you for an hour; your mom said you were on your bike. It wasn't safe for you to be out; I was worried. If I hadn't spotted Ryan . . ." He stood on the brakes and slid all the way across the parking lot.

On the grass, Rita had her twin in her arms. Eddie was trying to pull her away, but broke off as Steve erupted from the car toward him. Eddie ran down the path that led to the old boathouse. Steve went past Ryan and Rita without breaking stride, trying to catch Eddie.

Alice reached the top of the path and stopped, her breath still coming in ragged gulps. Steve had left the path and cut across the slope, closing the gap. As Eddie ran along the water's edge, past the old dock, Steve reached a point on the slope a few feet above him. He dove headlong for Eddie and momentum carried both of them across the dock and into the cold water.

As they splashed into the lake, Eddie screamed—a high-pitched sound of pure terror. Alice choked on a half-sob. She'd gone diving off the dock last summer; the water was at least twelve feet deep. And Eddie couldn't swim.

She reached the dock and dove in without stopping. The biting cold of an October lake left her gasping as she came up for air. She looked around wildly. Farther out, the splashing made Eddie and Steve look like two little boys having a water fight. She swam for them, knowing the truth was much grimmer.

She reached Steve's side just as he broke the stranglehold Eddie had on him. Eddie was beyond thought, the panic of drowning making him as dangerous as a frenzied shark. He clutched at Steve again, almost pulling him under. As Steve broke his grip, Eddie slipped under the surface.

Steve grabbed her arm, treading water.

"Careful! He was trying to pull me under." He looked around, waiting for Eddie to reappear.

"He can't swim!" she screamed. Steve looked at her blankly for a second, then, with a curse, he dove. She gulped air, still feeling the burning in her lungs, then dove herself, searching for Eddie.

By the time they found him and dragged him to the surface, it was too late. Steve towed him ashore, and they took turns attempting artificial respiration, but it was no use. Eddie was dead.

Steve finally pulled Alice away. "Come on. Leave him for the police." She was shaking so hard she could hardly stand, and Steve wasn't in much better shape. They stumbled up the path together, holding each other up.

Rita was still hugging Ryan when they reached her. Alice looked down at him and fought back the bile rising in her throat at the sight of his blood. But against all odds, he wasn't dead. She didn't realize it until he spoke.

"Alice." It was a whisper, almost beyond hearing, but she fell to her knees beside him. His eyes were open, half focused, drinking in the sight of her face. "Alice. You're alive."

"Oh, Ryan." Dimly, Alice became aware that the tears had started quite some time before. "You saved my life, Ryan."

She slipped an arm around Rita, embracing them both. Rita shuddered, then raised her head. Her face was distorted by all the hysterics of the past few hours, but she was coming back to sanity.

"Eddie?" The question held the remnants of terror.

"He's dead."

Rita nodded. There was no need to explain how; their wet clothes told the whole story. She said, in an almost normal voice, "If it hadn't been for us, your life wouldn't have needed saving. It started as a game, almost. Things just got out of hand. I should have known that with Eddie, it would end like this no matter what."

Ryan's whisper came again. "Alice." She reached out and stroked his cheek gently. "Alice. I'm sorry. I love you."

His eyes closed as he passed out. Behind her, Steve tried to pull her to her feet. Alice sighed, then stood up as she realized that her long nightmare was over.

SEVENTEEN
Epilogue

Detective Higgins held the door open for Alice as she entered the hospital room. Ryan was awake. He was almost as pale as the pillowcase his head rested against, but at the sight of her there was a flash of joy in his face. It went as quickly as it had come, replaced immediately by wary caution. In the visitor's chair against the wall, a uniformed officer eyed her and Higgins with interest.

She turned to Higgins. "Please? You did say I could be alone with him. . . ."

Higgins nodded once, sharply. He jerked his head toward the hall and told the man, "Wait outside."

The policeman got to his feet and left the room. Higgins looked at Ryan, then told Alice, "No more than fifteen minutes, and the door stays open." Then, with another look at Ryan, he left, shutting the door halfway behind himself.

Alice awkwardly handed Ryan a get-well balloon. The hospital room was unnaturally barren of such objects—no cards, no balloon bouquets, only some flowers from his family. It wasn't too surprising. Most people would feel uncomfortable sending flowers to an accused murderer.

"Thanks." He read the simple message, then held the ribbon tightly in his fist. There was silence for several minutes. "How are you, Alice?"

"I'm fine." She had fought to get this time alone; now she didn't know what to say. She made an unnecessary fuss about pulling the visitor's chair up beside the bed.

"How did you manage to swing this, anyway?" He broke the ice. "I didn't think they'd let me have private visitors."

She laughed, a little shakily. Suddenly she relaxed. No matter what, he was still Ryan, not some fire-breathing monster. She could talk to him. "I asked and Detective Higgins said yes. I embarrass him. He was so sure about me, and he was so wrong. . . . I think the city council felt the same way. They called a special session just to reinstate my scholarship, and they passed a resolution commending me for good citizenship. I guess just for an apology, I didn't earn it."

"They gave the scholarship back?" He smiled broadly. "Hey, terrific!" For a moment, the shadows retreated, and it was as though the past two weeks had never happened.

"I've talked to Rita on the phone," Ryan said. "She's out on bail, but she's not leaving the house. I was afraid she'd have a breakdown, but she's going to make it. We both confessed, and I think they'll take it easy on her. She didn't do that much."

"Ryan, why did you do it? And why did it keep looking like I was behind it all? I thought I was going crazy."

He looked down at the foot of the bed. When he spoke, it was to the footboard, not her. "I always thought I'd make a good master criminal. A game, you know? Moriarity, a hotshot European jewel thief . . . I was bored. School was a drag, and nothing ever happened here in Anslow. So I started playing a game with Eddie. At first, all we did was try to figure out how we could pull off the perfect crime."

He stopped and pain washed across his face quickly. "Only it stopped being a game for Eddie a long time before I realized what was going on. I knew he'd been having fights with Rita, but I didn't know it was because he'd gotten into drugs. He had, and he started knocking her around. If she'd told me then . . ." He slammed his right fist down on the mattress. In his left, forgotten and incongruous, he still clenched the purple ribbon of the balloon.

"His folks were getting suspicious of how much he was spending; he needed the money. And he had Rita scared, so she egged me on. I had it all set up, but we needed a patsy. And then . . ." he swallowed hard and went on. "Then Eddie jumped the gun. For some reason, he broke into the Larkins' place on his own. He was high and I think he thought it was a game. We kept thinking it was all just a damned game."

She looked away. The pain in Ryan's face could draw blood. He went on, still talking to the foot of the bed, while she fastened her eyes on the cheerful multicolored balloon.

"That was why he tore things up—fun. But two things happened. I was at the Senior Startup, so I had a nice, solid, prominent alibi. And I met you."

He reached out and took her hand. Startled, she looked down. He still held the ribbon, caught now between their hands.

"You were special, but I was still looking for a patsy. And you dropped that notebook of yours, remember? The one with all those baby-sitting jobs listed in it. I swiped it. I don't think you ever noticed it was missing."

"I . . . I don't remember. But why did you want it?"

He smiled, almost sadly. "Alice, it was a gold mine for us. Here we'd been wanting a patsy, and the notebook literally dropped into my hands. By blind luck, the Larkins were on your list. It was all there, names, addresses, when you usually sat for them. . . . I photocopied it, then I slipped it back into your knapsack. And I asked you out."

"That was all I was, then." She spoke quietly, through a tight throat. "Just a convenient sucker."

"At first." He raised himself up onto his elbows. "Only at first, Alice, I swear! But by the time I knew I was in love with you, we were in it too deep. I tried to back off, but Eddie wouldn't stop. I couldn't control him, and he kept getting worse about smashing things up. So I tried to get you out of it."

He fell back against the pillows again. "Only it didn't work. I planned to give you an alibi for the job at the Raineys'; that was why I made the date. Rita knew they were going to be gone, and they usually took the kid with them. You never told me you were supposed to be there. And we didn't expect Nancy. I tried to stop Eddie, but he was totally stoned. He always was when we pulled a job. And after that, everything just kept making it look worse against you."

"Coincidence." She'd been right, or nearly so. "Bad luck and coincidence." She shook her head.

"And Liz, don't forget her. That was when it really fell apart, when Liz started guessing and hinting and trying to blackmail Eddie. We never told her what was going on, but she pretty much had it figured out. Only she didn't know for sure who was involved, so she just kept accusing everybody. Especially you and Steve."

He stopped and squeezed her hand. "Remember all that candy she and Rita sold? That was my idea. They'd get into people's houses, and ask for the bathroom, or a glass of water, or whatever, and just poke around. Liz didn't really know what was going on, but she liked nosing into other people's stuff. After we got your list, they focused there. Rita found that pearl necklace at the Munsons'. And Eddie and I collected donations for the Athletic Club, doing the same thing."

"But why didn't the police figure it out?"

"What was there to figure? We didn't work together, and most people aren't going to remember a girl selling band candy who asks to use the bathroom. Especially not weeks later. There wasn't anything for the cops to get hold of." He gave a twisted smile. "My plan. I told you I'd make a good master criminal."

She squeezed his hand. "And Steve thought I was involved. He noticed the connection with my baby-sitting list even before the police did. And when he saw me stop at the Raineys' that night, he assumed I was sitting and he called there. He talked to Nancy. Only he didn't dare say anything about it to the police, because they were suspicious of him. And he thought I was framing him. It wasn't until I accused him of being the murderer that he realized I wasn't. He was furious, but after he calmed down, he figured I was in danger. So he followed me."

"Yeah. I owe him for that, a lot. If he hadn't, you and Rita would both be dead."

"And you."

"And me." Silence fell again. Then Alice looked at her watch. The time was almost gone.

"How . . . why didn't you stop him from killing Liz?"

"You think I wouldn't have?" Ryan struggled to sit up a little straighter. "I didn't even know. She was trying to blackmail him, and he didn't want to pay up."

Ryan stopped talking and lay back against the pillows again, pain etched across his face as he remembered. "I really was out renting a video that night. Eddie and Rita were heading for the lake and they saw Liz and picked her up." Ryan stopped, having trouble continuing with the gruesome story. "Liz started up again, and he killed her. Right in front of Rita. I got home and she was hysterical, and Eddie was threatening to make sure we'd both get arrested with him if we didn't back his alibi."

He stopped and closed his eyes. After a moment, Alice said, "I don't think they're going to try Rita as an adult. Higgins said so."

At that, Ryan's eyes opened. He tried to sit up, tears suddenly streaming down his face. His game was all too real now.

Alice looked into his eyes. "I don't know if they've made up their minds on you, but they know you stopped Eddie."

There was a soft knock on the partially opened door, and Higgins stuck his head into the room. "Ms. Fleming? I can only let you have a few more minutes."

She stood up.

"Alice," Ryan said, reaching for her hand again. "I'm sorry you got messed up in this. You're too special."

She leaned over and gently kissed his forehead. "Ryan, I'm sorry too. I'm not any more special than you, or Rita. Or Nancy, or even Liz and Eddie. I'm just sorry it started at all." She slipped her hand loose from his, and the balloon, its ribbon freed, floated to the ceiling. "Good-bye, Ryan."

She walked away from the bed. Higgins was waiting to escort her out. The next time she saw Ryan, it would be in a courtroom. At the end of the long hospital corridor, Steve, who had been waiting, joined her, and they left the hospital together.

Here's a sneak preview of the terrifying sequel to **The Vampire Diaries**
Volume IV: Dark Reunion

by L.J. Smith

Bonnie was sitting on lush manicured grass which spread as far as she could see in all directions. The sky was a flawless blue, the air warm and scented. Birds were singing.

"I'm so glad you could come," Elena said.

"Oh—yes," said Bonnie. "Well, naturally, so am I. Of course." She looked around again, then hastily back at Elena.

"More tea?"

There was a teacup in Bonnie's hand, thin and fragile as an eggshell. "Oh—sure. Thanks."

Elena was wearing an old dress of gauzy white muslin which clung to her, showing how slender she was. She poured the tea precisely, without spilling a drop.

"Would you like a mouse?"

"A *what*?"

"I said, would you like a sandwich with your tea?"

"Oh. A sandwich. Yeah. Great." It was thinly sliced cucumber with mayonnaise on a dainty square of white bread. Without the crust.

The whole scene was sparkly and beautiful. Warm Springs, that's where we are. The old picnic place, Bonnie thought. But surely we've got more important things to discuss than tea.

"Who does your hair these days?" she asked. Elena never had been able to do it herself.

"Do you like it?" Elena put a hand up to the silky pale-gold mass piled at the back of her neck.

"It's perfect," Bonnie said.

"Well, hair is important, you know," Elena said. Her eyes glowed a deeper blue than the sky; lapis lazuli blue. Bonnie touched her own springy red curls self-consciously.

"Of course, blood is important, too," Elena said.

"Blood? Oh—yes, of course," Bonnie said, flustered. She had no idea what Elena was talking about and she felt as if she were walking on a tightrope over alligators. "Yes, blood's important, all right," she agreed weakly.

"Another sandwich?"

"Thanks." It was cheese and tomato. Elena selected one for herself and bit into it delicately. Bonnie watched her, feeling uneasiness grow inside her by the minute, and then—and then she saw the mud oozing out of the edges of the sandwich.

"What—*what's that*—?" Terror made her voice shrill. For the first time the dream seemed like a dream, and she found that she couldn't move, could only gasp and stare. A thick glob of the brown stuff fell off Elena's sandwich onto the checkered tablecloth. It was mud all right. "Elena . . . Elena, what—"

"Oh, we all eat this down here." Elena smiled at her with brown-stained teeth. Except that the voice wasn't Elena's; it was ugly and distorted, and it was a man's voice. "You will, too."

The air was no longer warm and scented; it was hot and sickly sweet with the odor of rotting garbage. There were black pits in the green grass, which wasn't manicured after all, but wild and overgrown. This wasn't Warm Springs. She was in the old graveyard; how could she not have realized that? Only these graves were fresh.

"Another mouse?" Elena said, and giggled obscenely.

Bonnie looked down at the half-eaten sandwich she was holding and screamed. Dangling from one end was a ropey brown tail. She threw it as hard as she could against a headstone, where it hit with a wet slap. Then she stood, stomach heaving, scrubbing her fingers frantically against her jeans.

"You can't leave yet. The company is just arriving." Elena's face was changing; she had already lost her hair, and her skin was turning gray and leathery. Things were moving in the plate of sandwiches and the freshly dug pits. Bonnie didn't want to see them.

"You're not Elena!" she screamed, and ran.

The wind blew hair into her eyes and she couldn't see. Her pursuer was behind her, she could feel it right behind her. Get to the bridge, she thought, and then she ran into something.

"I've been waiting for you," said the thing in Elena's dress, the gray skeletal thing with long twisted teeth. "Listen to me, Bonnie." It held her with terrible strength.

"You're not Elena! You're not Elena!"

"Listen to me, Bonnie!"

It was Elena's voice, Elena's real voice, not obscenely amused nor thick and ugly, but urgent. It came from somewhere behind Bonnie and it swept through the dream like a fresh, cold wind. "Bonnie, listen quickly—"

Things were melting. The bony hands on Bonnie's arms, the crawling graveyard, the hot, rancid air. For a moment Elena's voice was clear, but it was broken up like a bad long-distance connection.

". . . he's twisting things, changing them. I'm not as strong as he is . . ." Bonnie missed some words. ". . . but this is important. You have to find . . . right now." Her voice was fading.

"Elena, I can't hear you!" Elena!"

". . . an easy spell, only two ingredients, the one I told you already . . ."

"Elena!"

Bonnie was still shouting as she sat bolt upright in bed.

📖 HarperPaperbacks *By Mail*

Read all of L. J. Smith's spine-tingling thrillers.

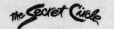

This new series from the bestselling author of The Vampire Diaries tells the thrilling story of Cassie, who makes a startling discovery when she moves to New Salem: She is the last of a long line of witches. Now she must seize her power or lose it forever....

THE VAMPIRE DIARIES
by L.J. Smith

The romantic, terrifying chronicle of a dark love triangle: two vampire brothers and the beautiful girl who's torn between them.

**Volume I:
THE
AWAKENING**

**Volume II:
THE STRUGGLE**

**Volume III:
THE FURY**

**Volume IV:
THE REUNION**

Look for:
TEEN IDOL
by Kate Daniel

Volume I: THE INITIATION
Volume II: THE CAPTIVE
Volume III: THE POWER

- - - - - - - - - -